IT W*** BLOOD

He drove the jagged glass into Harry's eyes.

And he ran.

He hadn't wanted to kill Harry. But Harry was in his way. And nobody must be in his way. Not until he had got to Ruth, his Ruth. But before he found Ruth, there was the subway guard, and suddenly there was blood on both of them, and the guard was dead. He hadn't wanted to kill the guard, but…

But he had to kill them all. All the damnable interfering slime who kept pushing at him and telling him what to do and making him so confused and so mad.

And then he had Ruth in front of him, in the bedroom, and he knew what he wanted, but they wouldn't let him, they wouldn't let him—

And he had to kill again…

FOR A COMPLETE SECOND NOVEL, TURN TO PAGE 133

POLICE LINEUP:

VINCE
The pressures of being a world famous concert pianist got to him…and he snapped.

RUTH
She was a sweet and beautiful woman, but she unwittingly enticed the wrong sort of man.

BOB
Steady and dependable, his only mistake was marrying the perfect woman.

JANE
This tart was way too much for any man to handle. Dissatisfied with her husband, she made designs on her best friend's.

STAN
As a concert planner he was the go-to-guy, but in his home life he was a bit of an invertebrate.

SAUL
A car accident had destroyed his hands, along with his ability to play the piano, leaving him a bitter tyrannical father.

FURY ON SUNDAY

By
RICHARD MATHESON

ARMCHAIR FICTION
PO Box 4369, Medford, Oregon 97504

1:00 a.m.

There was moonlight on his face and he was playing a funeral march. But there wasn't any piano. There was just the cot he was lying on, low and narrow, without any bedding except a coarse brown blanket wrapped tightly around the mattress. He lay on the blanket, fully clothed, his head resting on a thin pillow. The wide shaft of moonlight flooding across his body lit up the whiteness of his lean hands while they played Chopin on his legs. There was silence in the ward but he heard the music in his head.

He was a young man, about 26 years old, with tangled black hair and dark eyes. His face was the work of a sculptor who had forgotten to stop at the right place; who had, in attempting perfection, overdone the job, cutting everything to paper thinness—ears and nostrils that seemed liable to tear, and lips and chin like brittle glass that might shatter at the slightest blow. And all white—alabaster, ivory white.

He lay straight on the mattress, the grey-flannel trousered legs stretched out so taut that the heels of his ankle-high shoes pressed against the railing at the foot of the bed. His chest, covered by a shirt of grey flannel, rose and fell slowly and evenly.

Breathe correctly, Vincent. You must have the breath control of a distance runner.

The eyes that had been staring at the high ceiling now closed tightly. The hands were transformed to white spiders that jumped on his legs, gouging and scraping out music.

Not triple f, Vincent, double f, for the love of God!

The dirge crashed in his ears and the chords echoed down the endless passage of clouded darkness that was his brain.

Now the slow reflective passage came to life beneath his fingers, consoling. He opened his eyes again to stare at the ceiling.

He was waiting for Harry. Harry was the male nurse who handled the ward, an ape of a man with plastered down hair and fat hands with black hair on their backs. Lying there, Vince thought about those hands while his own rippled gently over the keyboard that wasn't.

Harry's hands weren't piano hands, Vince knew. Harry had ape hands that were coming soon to pluck him from the darkness. He could almost see Harry moving down the outside hall for the door that led to the ward. He could almost see the door opening and Harry standing there, waiting for him.

His hands punched down and a crescendo of despair mounted in his brain. He didn't want to think of Harry so he pushed aside the thought of his moist searching hands, the vacuous smile. He jammed his eyes shut and propelled himself back to Town Hall. The audience was rapt. They held their breaths while he ended the funeral march, paused dramatically, then drove himself into the incredible fury of the last sonata movement.

Now he was really there. He had driven away all memories. There was no Ruth in his life. No Bob. No Stan or Jane. No Saul. He was alone with his music: the music that had always been his only comfort. He was bent over the keyboard, brow glistening with sweat, hands a blur of white movement on the keys, drawing out crystal sound from the stillness. Faster and faster. The sound of the music welled up in his brain.

Then the little man who had stabbed his wife sixteen times with a carving knife began to cough.

Vince's hands snapped into fists that trembled in the moonlight. His teeth clicked together and his body shuddered on the bed. The need for violence pushed out from his insides until he felt as if it would force out the walls of his body. It came on him like this, his temper. It came pounding up from his guts, eager for destruction.

Vince rolled onto his stomach and clamped his teeth on the pillow.

Vincent, you simply must control your temper!

A hissing breath escaped his lips. The memory of forgotten words only made it worse. He tossed onto his back and pushed up to a tense position, eyes wide open, planning to rush down to the little man's bed and squeeze the coughing from his lungs.

Then the man stopped coughing and went back to sleep. Vince caught himself, waited a moment, then fell back on the pillow. After a moment, he smiled in the moonlight.

Not now. Not when his chance was here at last. He'd waited too long to throw it away on a moment's vengeance. His breathing slowed down and he cleared his throat softly. I can control myself. I'm sane. That's the difference between a sane man and an insane man. When you're sane you have control. He smiled again.

Then he rolled on his side and looked toward the door that Harry would open soon. The door that led out to freedom. To revenge.

Madhouse, he thought, and his fingers tinkled a witty improvisation on his legs. They thought him mad. That was their mistake. Did the truly mad plot escape the way he did, with detail and care? No, not the mad. They gibbered and beat fists on the plaster walls and kicked at the door until Harry came. But they never planned like this.

He kept his eyes on the door, his hands drawing at each other as he waited. In his mind he went over the plan again. It was very simple. Once he had escaped he would leave the building and take the subway down to 18th Street. Walk a few short blocks in the early morning when the streets were deserted. Ring the bell, go upstairs, and wait outside the door. Then when Bob came to the door...

His knuckles cracked as he drew his hands into fists.

But what if Ruth came to the door first? His brow knitted at the sudden problem. Then he nodded curtly to himself. Never mind that. She'd understand why he was there. She wouldn't stop him. After all, wasn't she as much a prisoner as he was? Maybe she wasn't behind locked doors but she was a prisoner anyway. Held in a more vicious kind of chains, the chains of emotional terror.

Poor Ruth. She'd suffered long enough. Well, he'd take care of her. After Bob was dead they could go away somewhere together. He could get a job doing something. He had strong hands. Maybe he could play the piano in a bar at night when no one could see his face. But that didn't matter. It wasn't important that he played the piano anymore. He made a soft, scoffing sound. What was piano music to compare with his love for Ruth?

Yes, that was the plan. The long wait was ended.

Escape, revenge, escape, revenge, es...

He was up like a hungry cat at the slight clicking in the door lock. He crouched in the shadows by the bedside, licking the sweat drops from his upper lip.

The door opened.

Harry stood there square and white. Vince remained motionless, hearing in his brain thumping piano music beneath the liquid voice of the male nurse. The voice that always made Vince feel as if hands were massaging syrup into his brain. *You like Harry, don't you Vincie boy? Harry likes you. You're a nice little boy and Harry will take care of you.*

Vince took a deep breath and stood up. He started to walk down the aisle between the beds. Harry stood motionless, waiting. Vince's stomach muscles were tense at the sight of him. His fingers bent over into tight arcs at his sides. He moved stealthily through the ward of the sleeping mad. He didn't want any of them to wake up and start a disturbance. Everything had to go right.

He walked by the next window and the moonlight bathed him in its whiteness.

Then he started violently as a low chuckle sounded in the darkness at his left. His black eyes darted over and he saw Kramer sitting up in bed watching him. Vince stiffened, but he kept walking. He wouldn't stop now. If Kramer tried to stop him, then Kramer would die. He kept on walking and Kramer only chuckled again as if he knew something.

Vince smiled to himself. Well, let the fool chuckle. If he only knew that Vince would be out of the place soon, he'd stop chuckling soon enough.

He looked at Harry. Harry wouldn't stop him from escaping either. No matter how strong he was. Vince thought of raking out those watching eyes and stamping on them. He'd scrape them out the way he'd scraped Jane's face that night when she tried to seduce him. The way he'd tried to do with Saul that day before the maid had come in and found them.

Harry stepped back and Vince stood nervously in the hallway. He heard the door shut behind him and the sound of it shutting away his prison was like a chord of triumph.

He padded along quietly beside Harry, controlling his urge to twist away from the moist hand that lay on his shoulder, the heavy arm pressing across his back. At his sides, his hands still ran over his legs with menacing glissandos. They hovered and waited.

Build to the climax, Vincent! Build to it!

"Did you wait long for Harry, Vincie boy?"

Vince made a sound of assent. Be quiet, he told himself. Harry mustn't suspect anything about the escape.

"That's good, boy. I like your spirit. I told you I'd take care of you. Didn't I?"

Another sound of assent.

"Speak up, Vincie boy, speak up. Nothing to be scared of. We're gonna have a nice time, you and me. A few smokes, a coupla shots of whiskey, and—who knows?" He jabbed his elbow into Vince's side. "Eh, Vincie, boy?"

Vince nodded. He didn't hear what Harry was saying. His eyes kept moving down to the end of the hall. There was an office there. Vince remembered when they brought him there he had sat in the office and been fingerprinted. There was a guard there, too, and the guard would have a pistol.

"Whoa, there. Where you goin', Vincie boy? This is Harry's room right here. You think you're out for a stroll, boy?"

The voice was slightly menacing. Vince smiled as if he didn't hear the menace. He waited quietly while Harry pushed open the door and gestured for him to go in. He entered the small room and heard the big male nurse follow him in. He saw the dim bulb burning overhead. Then the door shut, the lock clicked and Vince's throat moved. He pressed his thin lips together. If he failed, he'd kill himself.

"Sit down, Vincie boy. Take a load off your feet."

Vince turned and looked at Harry's face, the pink, smooth skin, the fat sweat drops under his nose.

"I said, sit down, Vincie boy," the voice warned gently.

Vince sank down on the bed that had its covers thrown back. His hands flinched on the cool sheet. His eyes moved to the bedside table; to the half empty whiskey bottle on top of it, its cap off and lying beside it; to the open pack of Chesterfields. They didn't get cigarettes in the ward. Vince licked his lips.

"You want a butt, Vincie boy? You want one?"

Vince swallowed. He nodded once.

"Well, go ahead, boy. Have a butt on Harry. That's all right."

Vince reached for the pack. Harry's hand closed over his.

"You remember favors, don't you—boy?" Harry said. "When a pal does you a favor you remember it, don't you?"

Vince looked blank. Harry patted his cheek and nodded, chuckling.

"Sure you do, Vincie boy. When a pal does you a favor, you remember it. Take one, Vincie boy. Light up. Enjoy yourself."

The fumes tickled deliciously in his throat and nostrils. *Time,* he heard a voice, *you need time.* Over the glowing tip of the cigarette, he looked around the room at the closet, the bureau, the throw rug on the floor.

Then there was a rustling sound and Vince, looking up suddenly, saw that Harry had pulled off his white, short-sleeved shirt. His face tightened.

"What's the matter, Vincie boy? Take it easy. Harry won't bite your head off. Harry is your pal, remember?"

Vince looked bleakly at the dark swirls of hair that covered Harry's chest, the fat ridges that pushed over the belt line.

"Relax, Vincie boy. You're on a picnic, a regular picnic."

Harry's voice dripped like honey. But Vince had heard the same tone in his voice the time Harry had crushed in an old Italian's nose with one blow. Vince remembered the scream. He remembered the writhing body on the floor. A shiver passed over his body. He'd have to wait. He sat there smoking and his right hand played Scriabine and didn't know.

"How about a little pick-me-up, Vincie boy? You drink, don't you? Sure you do. There's nothing like a nice little pick-me-up to get us girls acquainted."

The amber liquid gurgled into the two glasses as Harry poured. Vince watched the hands. He was thinking of how Harry had watched him for a long time. When the men took their showers and Harry stood in the doorway to see there was no trouble, Vince had seen the male nurse watching him, running his eyes over the smooth leanness of Vince's body, the small, hard muscles, the firm stomach.

Once when McCarran had shoved Vince so he fell down on the icy wet floor, Harry had stepped quickly through the stinging sprays of water to spin McCarran around and drive his beefy fist into the Irishman's stomach. Then Harry had leaned over and helped Vince up and pretended to lose balance, pulling Vince's wet body against him.

Vince re-focused his eyes on the glass held before him. Even breath drained from his thin nostrils. *That's it,* he heard the whisper in his brain, *control your breath. That shows you're sane. No matter what happens you're going to get out of here.*

"Drink up, Vincie boy. Good for you. Puts hair on 'em."

Vince didn't take the glass. He knew he should drink to set Harry at ease. Yet he knew he mustn't touch it. Vaguely he recalled a time when that same dark liquid had stultified his brain and his reflexes. That was the night of the big party, he remembered, the one Stan threw after the concert at Carnegie. And Jane had taken him into the bedroom with her. No, drink was bad; he mustn't drink because he had no escape.

"I said drink, Vincie boy."

Vince shook his head, smiling.

Harry's face went blank.

"You're not drinking, boy?" he said flatly.

Vince stared at him. He felt his heartbeat catch suddenly.

Then a cry broke from his thin lips as Harry grabbed him by the hair and jerked back his head. Vince clamped his teeth together before Harry could pour in the whiskey. He could smell the nicotine breath of the big nurse, and the red face blotted the ceiling from sight.

"I said *drink,* you dirty little bastard!"

Vince twisted away with a whine and Harry, strangling on a curse, flung the contents of the glass in his face. Vince gasped and blinked as the whiskey burned in his eyes. Tears sprang from beneath the lids to mingle with the drops of whiskey on his face.

Harry shoved him onto his back.

"Awright, damn it," he growled, "cut the crap. I know what you are, so *cut* it!"

Vince tried to sit up, but the nurse, with one hand, pinned him down by the throat. Vince forgot his plan completely. He started to thrash violently on the bed, forgetting everything but the wild need to escape. He clawed at Harry's eyes and his nails scraped across the hot forehead. Harry cursed and something hard exploded against Vince's jaw. The sound of Harry's breathing flooded away and, when he tried to open his eyes, the red face was hazy before him.

"You want to fight, huh?" the words came through a fog. "Don't you know you ain't foolin' me? You ain't foolin' Harry for one minute, *Vincie* boy. I know you like it. Don't you, boy, *don't* you?"

Vince jerked away from the whiskey-laden breath.

He whimpered in fright and a voice crackled in his brain.

Dear boy, do go to the bathroom and wash off your face. You look positively bizarre.

Harry's hands started to move over him. The pain in Vince's jaw made him groan. His struggles began to weaken. Then he shuddered violently as Harry started to unbutton his shirt. The moan in his throat rose in volume.

"Aah, shut up, boy! You know you like it." The red face leaned close and the obscene breath covered Vince's mouth and nostrils.

Vince closed his eyes. All he could think of was three words. They drummed into his brain again and again.

When it's over, when it's over, when it's...

*   *   *

He opened his eyes. The sound of bubbly snoring filled his ears. He sat up quickly and slid his bare legs over the side of the bed.

He stood looking down over Harry. On his flesh he still felt the bruises and teeth marks. As he stood there, breathing evenly, his hands moved on his stomach as if they were rubbing off something.

His mouth tightened. Well, it was over now and he was one step closer to freedom. His plan had worked. Harry was dead drunk. Vince had seen to that. He'd needed an advantage and now he had it. Smiles and touches had made the male nurse drink all of the whiskey, leaving Vince clear-headed and strong.

Now he reached out as if he meant to start the opening chords of the Rachmaninoff Second. But instead of music he drew an empty whiskey bottle to himself. He stood there motionless over the bed, looking down. Then, with a sharp motion, he broke the bottle in half across the table edge. Harry stirred and mumbled to himself and Vince heard someone screaming in his brain. *If you dare touch his hands, I swear I'll kill you!*

Vince leaned over Harry, his eyes glittering in the light of the bedside lamp. He rolled the bottleneck in his fingers. Then, abruptly, the color drained from his face and a trembling pulled back his lips. He tapped Harry on the shoulder.

"Wake up, Saul," he said.

And, when the sleep-thickened eyes fluttered open for a second, he raised his arm and drove the jagged glass edges straight down into them.

1:15 a.m.

Bob looked up from his work as the kitchen door swung open and Ruth came in carrying a tray with sandwiches and milk. She was wearing her pink quilted robe and her blonde hair was drawn back in a ribbon-knotted horse's tail. She smiled at him as she moved across the rug.

He put down his blue pencil.

"Honey, you should be in bed," he scolded her.

"If you can work until one o'clock Sunday morning I can stay up to feed you."

She set down the tray on the card table over the sheaf of papers he'd been working on.

"There," she said.

He smiled tiredly and stretched.

"You look cute," he said.

She leaned over and kissed him on the nose.

"That's for flattery," she said.

She got the hassock by the chair and drew it up to the table. Then she sat down on it and smiled up at him. A slight yawn parted her red lips.

"There, you *are* sleepy," he said. "You should be in bed."

"You're sleepy too," she countered. "Are you in bed?"

"I am the wage earner," he said. "The breadwinner. The proletariat."

"Eat."

He picked up a sandwich and bit into it.

"Mmmm. Good," he said.

"How's the work coming?" she asked.

"Oh, pretty good, I guess."

"Almost finished?"

"Just about," he answered. He sighed and reached for the glass of milk. He took a sip and put it down.

"I'm sorry we had to miss that dance," he said.

"Oh, don't be silly," she said. "Anyway—I guess I won't be gallivanting around much anymore."

He grinned and patted her warm cheek.

"Little mother," he said.

Then he leaned over and kissed her on the mouth.

"I taste mustard," she said.

"How romantic." He yawned again.

"I bet you say that to all the expectant mothers."

"Not all."

"All the girls then."

"Only those I love," he said.

"That would be—" she estimated, "Ava Gardner, Lana Turner…"

"Marie Dressler."

She made a tiny amused sound.

"How about Jane?" she said. "She's a hot number."

"She's an odd number," he said. "All she has is a body."

He grinned at her. Her face had fallen a little.

He knew what was bothering her. Ever since Ruth had become pregnant she would keep looking in the mirror searching for signs that she was getting fat. It bothered her. She always liked to look at her best for him.

"Well…" she said.

"Honey, you know you're the only one."

"She *is* sort of pretty," she said.

"Who, Marie Dressler?"

When she didn't answer he pulled her hair gently.

"Now cut it out," he said.

She took his right hand and pressed it to her cheek.

"I'm sorry," she said quietly.

"Okay." He finished the sandwich. "Speaking of that," he said, wiping his fingers on the napkin, "when is Stan going to wise up?"

She shrugged.

"I don't know," she said. "Poor Stan."

"Well," he said, "he made his own problem. He knew what she was before he married her."

"He never should have married her."

"That is the guess of the week," he said.

"I guess he still wants her, though."

"The world is strewn with the remains of men who wanted what they shouldn't have had."

She looked at her hands. "I suppose so," she said.

"He just ain't her speed," he said.

"Oh, he's not that old."

"Stan is forty-six and Jane is twenty-five. He's no Gregory Peck and she's a good looking woman."

She shook her head again.

"It's a shame," she said.

"Sure it's a shame. Hey, aren't you having some of this food?"

"No. I'd just get an upset stomach," she said. "You know about ladies in my condition."

He stroked her cheek once and smiled affectionately at her.

"What'll we call him?" he asked.

"Him. It's decided already?"

"Sure. A son for the McCalls."

She sat there smiling to herself.

"Maybe," she said.

He leaned over and kissed her.

"Love ya," he whispered in her ear.

Then he straightened up, selected a cookie, and bit into it.

"What was we talking about before we smooched?" he said. "Oh, yeah, I remember. Why Stan still hangs on the ropes."

"I don't know."

"He ought to ditch her. She's going to drive him out of his mind."

"You think it's that bad?"

"Sure it is," he said.

He smiled at the look on her face.

"I know, I know," he said. "You went to college with her and she's always been your friend. Well, you can't live in the past. Let's face it, she's a nympho. She'll sleep with anybody."

He reconsidered.

"Except maybe her husband," he amended.

"Oh, she can't be that bad. I won't believe it."

"Honey, anybody that would try to seduce Vince *must* be that bad."

Ruth looked down at her hands again. She thought about Vince for a moment. Vince, so young and so eager. And so damned.

"Poor Vince," she said. "It was a pity."

"I know," he said. "Well, Vince I can feel sorry for. That father of his."

He shook his head. Then he smiled cheerfully at her.

"Come on, let's get off the subject. How about a brief discussion on a name for our seven-month-distant heir?"

"Don't you have to work?"

"Oh, I can finish up in the morning. Right now I want to relax with my wife for a while."

A look of pleasure crossed her face. He got up and helped her to her feet. They walked over to the couch and she sat down. Then he went over to the record player, put on a record, and came back to the couch. As he sat down and put his arm around her the first strains of Ravel's *Daphnis* and *Chloe* filled the room.

Ruth cuddled close to him and laid her head against his shoulder.

He reached down and patted her stomach. "Comfy, Guiseppe?" he asked.

"Is that what we're going to call him?"

"Sure," he said. "Guiseppe McCall; that's a fine name."

"Guiseppe McCall," she said. "It has a ring."

They sat in silence awhile, listening to the music and thinking about their coming child. While she listened and dreamed Ruth looked up at her husband's face at his silky blonde hair, his straight nose, the strong chin line. She wanted to reach up and touch his slight beard. Emphatically, her right hand twitched in her lap and she made an amused sound at herself.

"Hmmm?" he asked.

"Nothing."

Nothing, she thought, it was a good deal more than nothing. It was rapidly coming to the point where she adored him.

Sometimes she thought that maybe it was the child, maybe it was an instinct for love and protection in a needful time. But then she knew she'd felt this way before she'd become pregnant too; pregnancy had only made it worse.

She was afraid that sometimes it was too obvious. She dreaded making a pest of herself; men never loved that kind of clinging woman, she was sure. And yet there wasn't a single detail of him that didn't fascinate her. She watched him dress, admiring his tall, muscular body, paying minute attention to each motion he made. Each morning she did that until he was dressed. Then she would rush into the kitchen and make breakfast.

She liked to watch him eat, enjoying the relish he gave each meal. She liked to watch him when he worked sometimes after office hours, bringing his briefcase full of papers to set out on the card table. She even liked to watch him shave; that's how bad it was. Watching him do everything gave her the feeling of absorbing him completely, every detail of him. It gave her a strange yet certain feeling of safety; as if she belonged to him and was protected from all bad things.

She sighed and pressed against him.

"Now what are we going to call him?" Bob asked.

"Who?" she asked.

"Our son."

"Mary?" she suggested.

"Not tough enough," he said. "What about George?"

She shook her head. "Uh-uh."

"Max?"

"Nope."

"Sam, Tom, Bill, Phil, Jim, Len, Vince—oops, sorry, slip of the tongue."

She didn't smile.

"Wonder where he is," Bob said.

"I don't know," she said.

She felt the other feeling now; the one that came whenever something was discussed that seemed to mar their happiness. It was silly to feel that way, she knew, as if she wanted to wear blinders or be like that sundial. What was the statement that went with it? *I record only the sunny hours.* Well, that was really silly. There was a lot of night in the world too.

But, at least, you didn't have to think and ponder about things that were all over with. There was only one person who could let her past with Vince hurt them and that was her. She mustn't dwell on the past as Bob said.

"I'll never forget that afternoon up in the agency," he said. "It was—crazy."

"Don't," she said.

"All right." He smiled and kissed her cheek.

They sat listening to music some more. He tried to forget it but the memory of that scene stayed with him. Sometimes he would jolt up from the bed in the middle of the night reliving it. The thunderstorm working alone in his office after a bad afternoon and then to top it all off...

He shook it off.

"Are we going to that party next Friday night at Stan's?" he asked.

"It's up to you, honey," she said.

"Well, there's no use lying; I don't particularly want to go. Stan's all right, but Jane gives me the creeps. I get the feeling she's going to explode sometime right in my face; a million pieces of Jane Sheldon flying all over the apartment."

"I get the same feeling," she said. "At college Jane used to throw herself around so much I wondered how she'd ever graduate."

"Did she?"

"In the top ten percent of the class."

"My God. Wouldn't you know it..."

He looked down at her and smiled as he stroked her soft hair. He shook his head slightly without her seeing it. How in hell she and Jane ever managed to stand each other's company for three years at college, he'd never know. They were so utterly different. Jane was a hand grenade with the pin out. Ruth was...

No, you couldn't pin a pat little metaphor on Ruth; she was too atypical.

Jane you could characterize. You could put her down in words. She was more like a taut spring than a woman, made of sharp lines and angles with no contour that was smooth or soft; stiff, high breasts, hips and buttocks flat and hard, and legs like taut pistons driving her on.

That was a woman, maybe, but not the kind of woman he wanted. It wasn't that he'd been brought up so strictly; not that he was a momma's boy who always sang within himself the old refrain of *I want a girl just like the girl...*

It was just that, after a man had lived a while, loved a while, been around a lot of women, he wanted a woman he could trust and be at ease with. One he could feel sensual heat with, sure; but not a heat that was so constant it started to consume. That was Stan's trouble. You couldn't burn at a constant heat without charring after a while.

No, you needed a girl you could relax with too. A marriage took place in all the rooms of an apartment.

Bob thought about the first time he'd met Ruth. He'd been doing publicity work on one of Vince's concerts. One night Stan, Vince's business manager, had held a party. One of those endless parties that seemed always to be going around Stan's beleaguered head. It was there that he'd met Ruth.

He had liked her appearance; the neat, unaffected way she dressed; the well-scrubbed facade she presented. He liked her smile.

But the thing he'd liked most was her complete difference from Jane. Jane was tight and hard, always brittle, always dashing around the party from one person to another, cigarette in one hand, cocktail in the other; always pushing so hard to be terribly clever and terribly gay. It was against the aura of pseudo-smartness that Ruth had stood out so strongly.

Was there a word that typified his Ruth? It wasn't *old-fashioned* because that had connotations of prudishness that didn't apply to Ruth. Maybe real was the word. She didn't try to impress anyone. And that was the secret of her impression on him. Even now, after three years of marriage, after long intimacies and discoveries, she was still something new and vital to him. And the fact that she carried within her a tangible part of him was something even more exciting and wonderful.

He tightened his arm around her and she grunted.

"Easy, strangler," she said.

He chuckled. Yes, with a wife like this he could even stomach *Hilton, Hilton, Joslyn and Ramsay; Advertising.* He thought about his office there, bright and clean, the grey wall-to-wall carpeting, the soft lights.

Then, all of a sudden, he was back to that day when Vince had come there. He hissed in disgust at not being able to rid himself of the memory.

"What's the matter, darling?" she asked.

"Nothing."

"Thinking about Vince?"

He looked at her in surprise. "How did you know?"

"Expectant woman's intuition," she said, half in amusement.

He sighed.

"He was quite a boy," he said. "I wonder what kind of a life you would have had with him."

"I don't even want to think about it. That temper..."

She slid her arms around him suddenly.

"I love you, Bob," she murmured.

Just the music undulating in the air. Bob pressed his cheek against her hair.

"I know sweetheart," he said. "I love you too."

They sat there on the big couch and listened to the record. Ruth looked around the room at the bookshelves, at the furniture. She kept trying to put Vince out of her mind. It was a terrible memory. She had been a small town girl fascinated by his lean good looks, by his smile, by his ability to play the piano. Only when she saw his temper did she realize it could never work out. And then Bob had come along...

The music ended.

"Bed?" he said softly.

"All right."

They rose leisurely and, while Bob turned off the phonograph, Ruth looked at what he'd been working on all night.

"Will it sell cars?" she asked.

"It better," he said, "or we'll have to put Giuseppe in an orphanage."

"He wouldn't like that."

"That's why this has to sell automobiles," he said.

"It will, honey."

Arms around each other they walked slowly across the room and he flicked off the light as they went into the bedroom.

1:50 a.m.

Vince crouched over the body of the unconscious guard and jerked the heavy pistol out of its holster. It felt good to have it in his hands, a solid comfort. When a man was excited and nervous he needed a crutch, and a pistol could be that crutch. A gun made him strong and it would frighten people. Most important it would hurt Bob. It would leave him dead—suddenly and completely—the way Vince wanted him.

His face twitched and his finger almost tightened on the trigger, so urgent was his desire to empty the pistol into Bob. The fact that Bob was so many miles away made Vince tremble with frustrated hate.

He straightened up and moved for the office door, anxious to get to the subway.

It had been ridiculously easy to overpower the old guard. The man had been sitting at the office desk half slumped over in sleep. Vince had only to pick up the lamp and smash it across his head. The old man had crashed back in the chair without a sound. Vince had dashed around the edge of the desk and now he was almost free.

He jerked at the heavy door that led to the outside hall. At first he couldn't believe that it wouldn't open. His eyes widened as if he was surprised. A questioning sound filled his throat. He pulled harder but the door remained fast. Vince's breath caught and he almost lunged against the heavy metal.

Then he stopped and held himself. It was not the time for temper. He had to escape. He closed his eyes. Why didn't the door open?

Then he opened his eyes. A key.

Now wasn't that terribly difficult to deduce.

His lips trembled as he moved back for the ·office. Always the voice of Saul in the background like an inescapable prompter hissing his cues from behind the dark curtain. No matter where Vince went no matter what he did, there was always some old remark of Saul's that would fit the occasion. His teeth gritted together. If only he knew where Saul was, he'd kill him too.

Vince bent over the guard again and felt through his pockets until he found the ring of keys. Then he returned to the door. He kept listening carefully while he tried one key after another. The hallway was silent, but in his minds ear he could hear, ludicrously, an old movie house piano playing "escape" music. It taunted him while he sweated over the lock.

Then the door opened. He was free. All he had to do was get down the stairs and out of the building. No one could stop him now. He gripped the pistol tightly.

The heels of his shoes were hard leather and they clattered on the metal steps. He had to slow down and hold onto the railing to ease himself down as noiselessly as possible. He put the pistol into his side pocket. It made a comforting bulge. Vince liked the pressure against his right leg.

Third floor. He stopped suddenly and his face went blank. Quickly he leaned over the railing and looked down. A gasp cut short his breathing.

There was an old woman coming up the steps carrying a scrub pail and mop, a bandana wrapped around her grey head. Vince stepped back hurriedly. If he went through the third floor door and waited there the old woman might go in there, too, and see him. He might even run into somebody else. But if he stayed on the steps, she might go up another flight and see him anyway.

Kill her! He clutched down at the pistol.

Once more he caught himself. *Don't be a fool.* A shot would arouse everyone. Especially in this stair well, it would echo all over the building. His head moved around as he looked for escape. A rushing of notes hung in his head like the beginning of a wild cadenza. The steps came closer— weary, trudging steps on the metal stairs. He backed against the wall and almost screamed out in hate.

It had always been that way. His temper had come over him like this. There would be a particular phrase to practice and Vince would work it over on the keys again and again, but still it wouldn't come. And his temper, like steam building up in a boiler, would keep growing, and finally, in a great roar, it would break out in a scream of frustration and he would double his fists and drive them like pistons into the keys. He would smash down clusters of black and white keys, making an endless chain of dissonances that would ring out in the penthouse apartment. He'd keep hitting even though his hands were bruised on the edges of the ivory keys and started to ooze blood. And he'd keep doing it until Saul came rushing in, screaming louder than Vince. He liked to do that, upset Saul. And the only way he could do it was to place those hands of his in some peril. It was the only thing that mattered to Saul about Vince. About anything.

And when the screaming and the pounding were done and he sat there at the piano heaving with sobs and unable to talk, Saul would make him start in again and perfect that phrase. And he always did. "Master technician." That was what the critics had called him. "The virtuosity of a Horowitz... No heart discernible but virtually unsurpassed for technique."

All of this flooded through Vince's mind as he pressed his lips together to keep the scream from flooding out. He was trapped. It was the feeling he always got. The world was closing in on him and he must kick and scream to be free of it.

Instinct drove him back up the steps to cower in the shadowed landing, halfway to the fourth floor. Instinct pressed him against the cold wall and snuffed out his breath.

Vince watched the old scrubwoman push through the third floor door. He watched the door swing slowly shut and thud into its frame. A smile relaxed his features. His hands lost their rigidity.

One more bow and then we'll get home to work on that Mozart phrase you desecrated this evening.

He moved down the stairs quickly, eagerly. In a half minute he was down to the first floor. He pushed open the door cautiously but the hallway was empty. Vince hurried down the length of it and reached the door. He pushed out through it and was on the street.

At first he wanted to stand there and stretch out his arms to the moon. The air was cool and delicious to the smell. He could have sung out in joy.

But there was no time; there was a thing to be done. Bob was still alive and, as long as he was, Ruth would be waiting to be freed. Vince started walking rapidly down the block alongside of the bleak grey building. He shivered a little in the cold morning air. How cool and clean it tasted after the smell of the ward with its unclean beds and the smell of many bodies crowded together.

Poor Ruth. Poor Ruth. Poor Ruth, his feet drummed on the sidewalk. He wondered if it was possible that Bob had drugged her. There had been that harmony teacher in Cincinnati, Vince remembered, who had kept his beautiful young wife under narcotics so she'd be faithful. His hands clenched together.

Ruth, Ruth! Her beautiful face twisted with pain—her lovely body profaned and—

He stopped thinking of that. He mustn't think of Ruth that way. She was purity and thoughts like that would spoil the memory of her. She was above that. So was he. They would live like brother and sister. They would!

Suddenly he realized he was standing still on the street holding himself stiffly. He hurried on. The subway, the subway, where was it? He'd only ridden it twice in his whole life. Once with Ruth just to see what it was like. Then another time when he and Saul had been stuck down in the Village somehow with no one to take them back to the penthouse and no cabs available.

Vince remembered that night as he walked along toward the corner. Saul had asked directions about ten times. And still they'd gotten lost and ended up in Columbus Circle. What a fool Saul was.

The cold began to seep through his flannel shirt. Suddenly he stopped again. What a fool he d been no to take a raincoat! Not only was it cold, but someone might recognize the grey flannel uniform of the maid. And the pistol bulged in his pants pocket.

He looked around and saw some darkened brownstone dwellings to his right. He looked into the lighted lobby and then he found himself jumping up the steps two at a time. He had to have a raincoat.

The vestibule door was locked. He looked at the names. *Martinez-3b, Johnson-3a.* They were no good. Vince skipped the names on the second floor too. He pushed the button under *Maxim-1a.*

He waited. There was no answer. They must be in bed, he thought. He pushed the button again, more impatiently. He had to have a raincoat. Still no answer. He began to wonder how he'd feel after he pushed the button to Ruth's apartment. He wondered just how he'd feel as he rode up the elevator with the pistol gripped tightly in his hand. He wanted that time to come, wanted it desperately. He felt angry frustration that he'd have to wait so long before it came.

The buzzer sounded. Vince started nervously, but forgot to push against the door. He tensed violently and almost kicked in the thick glass. Then the buzzer sounded again and he lurched against the door and pushed through it.

He moved quickly as a door down the hall opened a trifle. He ran to it and shoved his foot into the small opening.

"Open up," he said to the young woman who stood there.

She gasped and tried to close the door. His foot prevented her from doing it. Vince reached for his pistol with an angry motion and almost shoved the end of the barrel into her face.

"Do you want to die?" he asked in a hoarse whisper. The girl's face went white, her lips trembled, and she backed away from the door. He pushed his way in. The girl was cowering back against the wall.

"Don't," she said. "Don't do anything to me. Please don't."

She winced as he turned on the hall light. In the bright light Vince could see that her hair was disarrayed and there were red scars on her right cheek where she'd been resting on the pillow.

"Have you got a man's raincoat here?" he asked.

"What?"

"I want a man's raincoat," he snapped at her.

Then, without thought, he looked down over her pajama-covered body. His eyes moved back to her young breasts pressing against the yellow silk. He pinched his lips together. *No!* snapped his mind and, mocking, in the background came the voice of Saul. *My dear boy, if the pressure is annoying, relieve yourself. You don't need a woman for that.*

He felt a drop of sweat run into his mouth.

"Well?" he said angrily, forgetting for the moment what he was asking her about.

"I live alone here," she said. "I-I haven't got a man's raincoat."

His hand twitched at his side. He wanted to hit her for foiling him. He couldn't go to another apartment. He was getting that trapped feeling again. He'd always been that way. If he wanted something and couldn't get it the first time, he started to feel frustrated. That's how he felt now. He couldn't go to all the apartments when he had to get to the subway and get downtown. A fresh idea came to torture him; what if the guard regained consciousness and got the police out looking for him? Sooner or later he'd wake up and tell them. His breath grew restless; his finger trembled on the trigger.

"Get in the bedroom," he heard himself say.

He followed her in, wondering why he wasn't leaving. If there was no raincoat here, what was the point in staying? He fought against the ugly pressure in his body. He didn't like it. No, he wasn't that kind; that was insane.

"Turn on the lights," he ordered.

She stood by the rumpled bed, looking at him and shivering a little.

"What are you going to do?" Her voice was thin and afraid.

He didn't answer. Instead he went to the closet door as if he knew what he was going to do. He flung open the door and reached in, trying to avoid the sight of her slender body. She's sort of pretty, the thought rose unbidden in his mind. Blonde hair like Ruth. I'd like to—

He dug his teeth into his lower lip and turned to face the closet completely, not even looking at her. He reached in and came out with a black trench coat. He tried it on and it fit pretty well, and the cut wasn't too feminine. He'd have to chance it.

"Have you a telephone?" he asked, still not able to understand how he managed to think of all these details when his mind was so obsessed by the one desire to kill Bob.

"No," she said.

He wouldn't have to cut any wires then, he told himself and nodded once. Still he stood there not knowing what to do, his mind filled with a dozen questions. Should he leave the girl? Wouldn't she call the police? Should he shoot her? Wouldn't the people in the house hear the shot? Vince started to tremble nervously at all the disturbing elements that his coming in here had brought on. That was the trouble with life, no matter what you did it just made everything more confusing. *Kill Bob,* that was what he had to concentrate on. *Get to the subway and kill Bob.*

His eyes re-focused on the girl who still stood there watching him. He shouldn't kill her. She hadn't done anything to him. She was a pretty girl and she didn't mean him any harm. Only an insane man killed everybody. He only wanted to kill certain people like Harry and Bob. Harry was dirty and fat, and Bob was torturing Ruth. But that was all. There was Saul, too, but Vince didn't know where Saul was.

But he didn't kill the guard; he'd only knocked him out. Didn't that prove he wasn't crazy? His face softened without him realizing and the expression he directed at the girl was one of supplication.

"Are you sick?" said the girl.

Her tone and the words she used broke the spell. Vince's mouth tightened, his face lost all softness.

"I'll show you how sick I am," he said and pulled the trigger of the pistol.

There was a click. And suddenly, Vince felt cold sweat break out on his body. God, was he insane to make such a loud noise in this house? He gritted his teeth.

He had to save those bullets, too. He hadn't thought to look and see how many there were, but there could be no more than five. It was lucky that chamber was empty.

He saw that the girl was wavering as if she were going to faint.

"Get in bed," he told her.

She sank down weakly on the bed, her hands shaking in her lap.

"Get under the covers," he said.

"Wh—why—why?"

"I said get in bed!"

As she lay back the top of her pajamas slipped up and he saw an expanse of white skin. His heart pounded violently and he lowered his head an instant to hide the swallowing.

Hastily the girl drew up the blankets. She lay there watching him with glazed, frightened eyes.

"Close your eyes," he said.

She put her head down on the pillow and closed her eyes. Then a sob broke in her throat and she opened them again. Her voice shook.

"Are—are you g—going to hurt…me?"

"Close your eyes."

He moved closer, enjoying the feeling of power it gave him to hold life and death in his palm. He thought of killing Bob. He thought of how grateful Ruth would be when Bob was dead, how she would throw her arms around his neck and kiss him and …

"I said close your eyes!" he yelled.

He looked down at her white face. Then, abruptly he flung back the covers and stared down at her body. His hand moved down.

Get involved and you'll regret it, my fine young fool!

His hand jerked back. He threw the covers over her again and stood there looking down sullenly.

"I ought to kill you," he said. "You're not a clean girl. But I won't because I'm not as crazy as you think. Remember that if anyone asks you."

A breathless chuckle sounded in his throat.

They'll ask you all right," he said as casually as he could.

Then he bent over and kissed her on the cheek. Her eyes rolled up and she quietly fainted. He didn't notice.

Cheerio, he said and walked out of the bedroom and the apartment, feeling a pleasant sense of bravura he hadn't killed the wretched young nothing. He'd just taken her raincoat as any hero might, leaving her with a kiss on the cheek. That was heroic; it was the sort of thing a girl would remember. She wouldn't tell anyone. She'd treasure this experience because it was romantic. No, he hadn't, touched a hair on her head. That's because he wasn't insane. He'd just tried to kill his father that was all. Anyone might try to kill his father.

*   *   *

He stopped at the head of the subway steps and looked around.

There was no one following. As he had surmised, the girl hadn't screamed for help when he left. She was probably lying there and dreaming of the handsome man who had kissed her and stolen her raincoat. He smiled a smile of tragic acceptance and moved slowly down the steps.

Halfway down he stopped, the sense of poetry gone suddenly with the realization that he had no money. He stood there looking blankly down the steps. *This is absurd!* The words exploded in his mind.

His hand tightened on the gun butt. He wasn't going to let a ridiculous thing like this stop him. He walked down past the white tiled walls. He glanced at a seal balancing rye bread on its nose on one of the posters. Gust of the bizarre. That's what Saul would say. Vince wondered where he was, wondered if it were possible that someday they could get together again and get Vince back into concert work. Vince didn't like to admit it to himself sometimes, but he did miss the piano. He could tell himself that nothing mattered but Ruth and the piano was unimportant. But why did his hands always move over the keys even though he hadn't been near one in...how long?

Oh, what difference did it make where Saul was? Their lives were parted forever. Ever since that day in the penthouse. Vince remembered the rain; he remembered Saul backing away from him. *For the love of God, are you mad! Vincent!*

It was the only time he could ever remember his father calling him by his name.

He pushed again. Then he looked down curiously and saw that he was shoving futilely against the wooden turnstile.

Red flared up in his cheeks. Then he glanced hurriedly toward the change booth and saw that the man was looking at him.

Vince drew in his breath. The man started to open the door of the booth, and suddenly, Vince ducked down and darted underneath the turnstile. What if no train comes! He ran down the sloping floor, heart beating in fright.

"Hey, come back here, you!"

Vince reached the steps and jumped down them two at a time. The shouts of the man from the change booth echoed after him in the silent station.

"Come back here!"

Vince reached the platform and his eyes raced up and down the length of it. It was empty. He looked back up the steps to see if the man was following him. Then he leaned over the edge of the platform and looked out into the blackness to see if the train was coming. There was nothing. He looked up and saw that he was looking for the train that was going uptown. He moved for the other side of the platform, glancing at the stairs again.

"You ain't gettin' away, buddy!"

Vince gasped and his head twisted suddenly. He saw the man coming down the steps. He turned around and started running along the grey concrete. He heard the clatter of the man's shoes behind him. It was an older man with white hair, wearing a black coat sweater.

"You stop or I'll use this gun!" threatened the voice behind him.

Vince looked back over his shoulder and saw that the man held a small pistol. He started to whimper under his breath. The trapped feeling was coming over him again, starting from his stomach and spreading out with hot, twisting fingers.

"You want me to shoot you!"

Vince felt the gun banging against his leg as he ran. He saw the wall ahead of him.

"Now, you're caught!" said the man.

Something filled Vince's brain with night, because he wasn't aware of what happened then. He didn't even feel himself jerk the gun from the raincoat pocket. He hardly heard the explosions that almost coincided, that of his pistol and that of the man's. He felt someone strike him on the arm and knock him off balance. That was all.

Then he was looking at the scene as if he'd never seen it before. The man was writhing on the subway platform, blood gushing out of a great hole in his chest. Vince stared at him and then, as the man tried to raise his pistol again, Vince fired another bullet into him. The gun jolted in his hand and the sound deafened him.

The man lay dead on the platform. Vince looked down amazed at the smoke coming from the barrel of his gun. Almost repelled, he shoved the pistol into his pocket. He could feel himself shaking his head and murmuring something.

"I'm sorry," he said. "I *mean* it. I'm sorry."

Then the pain swept over him and he twitched violently. Looking down he saw blood running down the raincoat. He tried to lift his left arm and gasped at the fiery pain. His mouth fell open and a moan of fright filled his throat.

"No," he said. "No, no."

He looked incredulously at the man.

"He—he shot me," he said. He couldn't believe it. The man had shot him, he'd hurt him.

Then surprise and hurt flooded together into a hard, hot lump of hate. He fumbled for his gun again. But his hand caught in the lining and he couldn't get it out. Forgetting for a moment, he tried again to move his left hand.

The pain almost made him faint. He felt warm blood dribbling down over his wrist and into his palm. He stumbled around on the platform, waves of darkness lapping at his feet.

"No, no, no," he sobbed. "I don't want to."

He started sharply as a screeching whistle came from the black tunnel. The station grew more clear to his gaze. He found himself looking down at the dead man in horror. What if someone saw him? They would stop him!

"No!"

Without thinking, he grabbed the limp right hand of the man and dragged him along the platform leaving a trail of blood behind. His own left hand hung uselessly at his side. In a moment he'd dragged the body behind a refuse box. Then he hurried out and ran to the edge of the platform. He looked down and saw two white lights approaching and heard the far-off roar of the train. He shook his head to clear the mists from his eyes.

He looked down at his left hand. What if someone saw the blood dripping from the end of it? With his right hand, he hurriedly put the left into the raincoat pocket, gritting his teeth, his face white.

Then he stood there waiting nervously, his stomach throbbing spasmodically. What if they saw the man? What if they stopped him from getting to Bob? What if they saw his arm? He wanted to scream. What if he had no bullets left? What if the girl had called the police? What if the guard had regained consciousness? What if he bled to death?

He stood there shaking and whimpering in terror as the train moved past him, filling his nostrils with hot rushing air. It slowed down and the lights played on his white features.

The train stopped and he saw, with a shock, that there were several people in the train. What if they...?

He closed his eyes tight for a moment and tried to make his mind a blank. He heard the door open and he looked straight ahead as he moved into the fluorescent illuminated car.

He lurched back into the hard straw seat as the train started and couldn't stop the short cry of pain. His eyes moved nervously over the people. A man sitting across the aisle was looking at him. Vince lowered his head. He bit his lips to keep them from trembling.

He couldn't keep his eyes down. He had to know if anyone were looking at him. He glanced up cautiously. No one was paying attention. He took a deep, faltering breath. Then he leaned back and relaxed.

Maybe things weren't so bad after all. He had the raincoat and he was still on his way to kill Bob. If only—he closed his eyes and felt sweat break out on his forehead—if only the man hadn't shot him. The fool! What right had he to shoot him—all for a miserable ten cents? He kept his eyes closed and the motion of the train began to make him sick. Pain fled about his body, first localizing in his stomach, then in his head, but always coming back sharply into his arm.

The train slowed down and stopped at the next station. Vince felt the blood collecting in his palm. If it didn't stop it would start to drip on the floor of the train. No, it mustn't. He had to get to 18th Street, first. He looked out of the window. They were in the 80's. He closed his eyes again...

The doors closed and the train started. Vince drew in a ragged breath of the stale air. He opened his eyes and saw that a young Negro couple had come into the train. He looked blankly at them, sitting on the other side of the train and down a little ways. They weren't talking to each other. Vince's eyes moved to the girl's sweater she wore underneath a sport jacket. He swallowed and closed his eyes again.

A rattling sound filled his throat and he shivered violently. *It hurts!* Suddenly he thought of his playing. Would his left hand be ruined?

What's the difference? he told himself. *I've only got one thing to do that matters and that's to free Ruth.*

He started to remember about her. He remembered the party at Stan's where he'd met her. He remembered how they'd sat on a couch all evening and talked about music. She'd been so lovely and clean with her red knit dress and her shiny blonde hair with the ribbon in it. He had loved her from the start. Then later they had gone into the study and he had played for her. Then—he tightened at the remembrance—Jane had come in and spoiled it all, dragged them back into the noise and the smoke.

Clean, clean, clean. The wheels seemed to say the word as the train rushed through the black tunnel. Not like *her*. He closed his eyes. It was better she died when she did. If the car hadn't gone over the embankment someone would have killed her sooner or later the way she carried on.

Your mother was a bitch, pure and simple.

He stared at the floor dizzily. The noise of the train wavered in his ears and he had to keep blinking to keep the view before him from blurring. He swallowed. The air seemed hard to breathe.

His eyes fled across the train. He saw the Negro girl looking down at the floor beside him with a look of revulsion on her face. Quickly he looked down.

A small pool of blood was collecting near his left foot. He almost cried out.

He looked up and gasped as a man got up and started over. Vince shoved up and backed against the door. He drove his right hand into his pocket and gripped the gun. The man stopped and looked at him curiously, then his eyes moved down to the bulge in the coat and he backed away nervously. He bumped into the seat he had just vacated and fell down awkwardly.

Time seemed to stand still. Vince thought he'd scream. The train went on and on, and all the people kept staring at him. He wanted to kick his way through the door. He didn't care if he was flung into the blackness, but he couldn't stand to have all these people looking at him.

The train started to slow down. A station, he'd have to get off here. He had to have help. His teeth chattered and he felt a chill run through him. The train stopped and he almost fell out as the door slid open. He bumped into a young couple.

"Say, watch it, Mac," said the young man irritably.

Vince shoved past them with a sob. The young man said something he didn't hear and then the door closed. Vince staggered across the platform and was afraid he was going to fall. He heard the train start and saw that no one had followed him out of the car, although several of them were glued to the window looking at him with wide-eyed curiosity.

"Pigs!" he screamed, and was drowned out by the train.

He staggered further and collided with the tile wall. He leaned against it gasping for breath.

Then he saw a sign that read *Men,* and he pushed away from the wall and made his way to the doorway. He tried to push through the door. It was locked. He stood there staring at it. But he had to have some water! He started to cry and leaned his head against the cold metal while the tears ran down his cheeks.

After a while he drew his sleeve across his face and started walking along the station, ignoring the way the walls wavered before his eyes. *I'm going to kill him,* he kept telling himself. *I'm going to kill him.*

Stan.

2:30 a.m.

In dark stillness she lay starkly awake, her eyes fixed on the ceiling. Under the black silk of her nightgown her firm breasts rose and fell and her long white fingers drew in and out at her sides like the delicately pumping claws of a cat. Her red nails made a rasping, scratching sound on the sheet. Her mouth was a stark red line that did not move. Jane was twenty-five and her body lay like a taut spring, waiting for something.

Across the space between the two beds Stan groaned and rolled onto his side, complaining in his sleep. She listened to him rustling on the sheet of his bed, heard the weak thud as he hit his pillow once. Then he cleared his throat and was silent again. She did not look toward him; her eyes remained fastened on the dark ceiling.

He was probably sick again. He was always sick after a party. He drank too much and ate too much and made himself sick. Most men, when they drank too much, didn't eat at all. They filled their bodies with alcohol but took in no food to offset the breakdown of tissues. That's why drunkards died usually, she thought. That's why my dear old daddy died and left me the world he could never handle.

Her still painted lips pressed together now. She felt as if she had to have something fragile in her hands, something she could crush between her straining fingers.

For a minute she closed her eyes and tried to sleep.

She remembered how easy it used to be to sleep. Just a delicious exhaustion filling your body, just a closing of eyes and there you were. Now...

How could you sleep when your mind was like one of those toffee machines you see on amusement piers with those long arms turning and twisting, turning and twisting? Her brain was the toffee. She could almost visualize the metal arms twisting the great grey lengths of her mind. Desire twisted and folded over, frustration twisted and folded over. A deep sighing breath filled her lungs. Abruptly, she turned on her stomach and pressed her body into the bed. Her teeth gritted together and the column of her throat felt as if it were petrifying. God, to have Mickey Gordon in bed with her. Right now, here, even with Stan over there, what did she care? Or Johnny Thompson. Or Bill Fraser. Or Bob McCall, yes, that she'd like. Even if Ruth was her best friend. What was a friend for anyway?

Her white hands closed into tight fists. Her nails dug into her palms and she thought she was going to scream. Anyone! Even that gaunt and crazy Vince. Yes, maybe especially that gaunt and crazy Vince. That was what happened when you became a jaded connoisseur of the flesh, a jaundiced gourmet of love's old song—no longer sweet but in need of new spices. You tired of the plain fares, you wearied of the common menu. You craved something exotic, something new. And, in consequence, you positively threw up at the thought of your husband—at best, a tasteless mush.

She dug her nails into the sheets now and writhed her hot body on the bed until the gown had worked its way past her hips. *I'm going crazy,* she thought. *I'll end up like Vince. One night I'll get up quite calm and secure in my maniac shell and drive something sharp and final into the worthless corpulence I married.*

A rising, whining sound filled her throat. No, stop that, she demanded of herself. That sort of thing made Stan raise upon an elbow and whisper into the darkness his hateful, nauseous concern.

She had always thought of Stan in terms of an old nursery rhyme. Compendium of snails and puppy-dog tails—that was Stan, Mr. Sheldon. Snails for sluggishness of mind and movement. And puppy-dog tails—those flapping, flopping, rug-thumping indications of utter devotion, of adolescent, stomach-turning love. That was Stan too.

God, can't I stop thinking about him! her mind screamed. Oh, give me the empty, useless solace of a man's body here and now and let me forget the torture of mind.

In a minute she got up and went slowly into the living room. She felt her way among the glasses and plates strewn on the floor, feeling an occasional wet patch where some unstable reveler had dropped or spilled or kicked over his glass of whiskey and soda, or gin and soda, or vodka and soda or anything and soda. *Ploppo*, into the carpet. After the parties they'd had here, it was a wonder there was any carpet left at all.

She turned on the small lamp on the table beside the couch. She blinked and closed her eyes for a moment, then sank down on the couch and looked around the room.

She saw the end result of social tornado. Here in this penthouse, decorated by whosis of Fifth Avenue, furnished by what's-his-name and draped by the best non-entities in town—here, in this upholstered sewer, gaiety had reigned. People mixed drinks and company, told lewd jokes, crept searching fingers over the other men's wives and other wives' husbands. Flung the mud of their minds against the walls. Stole into darkened bedrooms for quick sensation. Let the gyroscope of their minds be swallowed under tides of liquor. Stumbled and laughed and threw up and screamed vile laughter and let the mask fall for an instant from the face of the beast. Showed the fangs and the hatreds and the endless lusts.

Jane reached over and picked up somebody's drink. I hope it was a man's drink, she thought and placed the glass to her lips. Cheap kiss, she thought, kissing a glass. As the warmish, watery liquor trickled down her throat the ultimate thought came—the party is over.

Oh God, come and take me, someone!

She wanted to scream it out in the silence of the apartment. She wanted to rip the flimsy gown off her body and give the sweetmeats of her flesh to any and all comers. Step up, line forms on the right. Jane Sheldon, wife of Stan Sheldon, has the pleasure of announcing her availability to all and sundry. Come one, come all.

She slumped down on the couch, shivering without control. Her hungry eyes ran down over her lean body, over the two hard points of her breasts, the flat stomach, the long perfectly shaped legs. She ran one hand over her stomach and it made her shudder. She finished the drink and sat staring into the empty glass, watching the tiny amber bubble on the bottom slide back and forth as she tilted the glass from side to side; slipping and gliding like a fat pig on a frozen lake.

Kill me, someone.

The thought crept into her mind, looked around, saw no resistance, and took over.

*　　*　　*

He had lain there and watched her rise. He had seen her standing in the living room. In her nightgown, the dark outline of her body showing against the lamp's glow he lay there in the dark bedroom staring at her, as she sat slumped on the couch. He watched her run a hand over her smooth stomach and something twisted in his guts. It had been so long, so horribly long. She never let him touch her anymore. They were married, but she never let him touch her.

She hardly even let him see her. Once In a while, maybe if she thought he was still asleep in the morning, she would let the nightgown drop rustling off her satiny body and, while she hooked and pulled and fastened and zipped through half closed lids he would drink in the sight of her breasts arching out from her chest, the flat smoothness of her stomach and buttocks, the curve of her legs. His own wife made him feel like a Peeping Tom, like some sub-species of voyeur.

His throat moved. Why didn't he go in there and just demand his rights? Why didn't he take her in his arms and conquer her resistance? The situation struck him in all its insulting absurdity.

Anyone else could have her but he couldn't.

He moved on the mattress and suddenly he froze, seeing that she was looking in at him. He lay there shivering while her eyes looked into the dark bedroom. He didn't think she saw him because she didn't say anything and, in a moment, she turned her head away. But for that moment, he had seen, in her eyes, how much she despised him. It had been no novelty. He saw it all day, too. But there was something faintly hideous about seeing it on her face when she didn't even think he was looking. It showed how ingrained her hatred was, how burned into her mind.

He lay there on his side looking with bleak, unhappy eyes at his wife sitting on the couch. He saw her finish the drink she'd picked up. Now she was staring into the glass, tilting it from side to side. What did she see in the glass? What was she thinking? Once he thought he had glimmers of her mind. Now she was more a stranger with each passing day. Once he could almost say they were in love. Now all he could say was that he paid the bills for the things she bought. And there were plenty of things.

A shudder made his muscles jerk abruptly and he closed his eyes to shut away the sight of her. No, he couldn't go in there and demand her body as if it were some patronage. He couldn't even talk to her.

Like some silly robot he would host her parties, pouring drinks, laughing at bad jokes, trying to ignore the sight of her on the couch or on a chair with some man, her open mouth writhing under his, her fingers raking across the man's back, that obvious dark flush filling her cheeks. Trying to ignore the moments when she would disappear and be gone from the living room. Then he knew that in the darkness of the bedroom, maybe on his own bed...

And he was a jellyfish. He could no more have gone in the bedroom when she was there with some man and confront them than he could have broken into the bedroom of the White House and demanded, *What the hell are you doing, Mr. President!*

He would go on pouring drinks and laughing at bad jokes and, maybe, if the pain in his flesh and mind got too unbearable he would make a faltering pass at some woman that no one else would make a pass at.

He started quickly to his elbow as Jane stood up and moved for the balcony.

He pulled back the covers, his heart thudding with fear. Everything was forgotten in an instant; his hate, his frustration, his despair. He was, once again, the simple, uncomplicated man who could do nothing but adore. Quickly he ran across the living room rug, his heavy body rocking from side to side, feet thumping on the rug. "Please don't, Jane. Darling, please don't. I'll make it up to you. I'll try to be what you..."

Jane turned from the railing and looked at him coldly.

"What do *you* want?" she asked, her voice flat.

The way she said *you*. It was a knife turning in him.

"I—I thought maybe..."

"Thought maybe I was going to jump?" she asked acidly.

"No," he said. "I mean, I just thought..."

She didn't say anything and they stood there looking at each other in silence in the early morning. She stood there on the terrace flagstones like Venus in Manhattan, like a debauched Aphrodite in a sheer Tiffany creation.

"Don't you think you should come in?" he said falteringly. "It's a little cold for just that."

"Just what?"

"I—I—that gown. I mean it's awfully thin."

Her eyes on him were like blue ice.

"You'll catch your death of cold," he offered.

"That would be wonderful," she said in a deceptive calm.

But, after a moment, she came in and went to the bar to make herself a drink.

He closed the French doors and stood there awkwardly, watching her make a drink that was nine-tenths whiskey. He swallowed and then straightened out the wrinkled twists of his pajamas. They were silly looking pajamas. He knew that. He often thought she bought them for him because she knew he would look ridiculous in them, with their little pink elephants sporting on the cloth.

"Place looks a mess," he said.

She didn't answer. She kept pouring whiskey.

"Guess—I'd better have the woman in Monday instead of Tuesday," he said.

She finished pouring her drink.

"How about another?" he said.

"Another what?" she said and sat down. Her nightgown slipped up over her knees and his throat moved. She looked up at him and pulled the gown up further, pleased at the mottled color it brought.

"You look like a cow in heat," she said idly.

"Maybe I'll have one too," he said, trying to ignore her remark.

"One what?" she asked.

She always asked questions like that. He knew very well she was aware of what he was talking about. But unless he named his object in so many words, unless he used the noun, she would impale him on a question he felt obliged to answer.

"I'll have a drink," he said in a surly voice.

"Sure, why not?" she said. "Drink up, dear one."

He didn't know how to take that sort of remark either. He rarely knew how to take her remarks. They always had the earmarks of a trap he might fall into. It made him nervous analyzing each of her remarks before he answered them. But he had to or else he wouldn't know what to say. And, anyway, he invariably stumbled and said the wrong thing and, suddenly, her scorn, or her mocking laughter, would surround him. Or, worse, her raw, nerve-taut fury would lash out at him and make him afraid. That was it. He was afraid of her.

He poured a little whiskey into a glass and squirted a lot of soda in after it. He knew he shouldn't have any. But he didn't want to go back to bed and he had to have some excuse to stay with her. That was the situation too. He had to have an excuse to stay with his own wife. As he made the drink he looked at his watch. It was nearly three o'clock.

He sat down in a chair across from her. "Couldn't you sleep either?" he asked, trying to be amiable.

"Sure," she said. "Sure I could sleep. I'm in there now. I'm sound asleep. This is my astral projection drinking whiskey of a Sunday morning. Astral projection of Jane Sheldon drinking whiskey. Corpus slumberi of Jane Sheldon asleep in bed, dead to sorry old world."

And what did you answer to such a remark? He insulted himself by smiling a little at her, sheepishly. He retained the smile but the muscles of his stomach knew, and they tied a knot that made him grunt and bend over in pain. A little of his drink spilled over the edge of the glass.

"Oh, for Christ's sake, go to bed," Jane snapped. "Don't subject me to your goddamn attacks!"

He straightened up and tried to blink away the tears of pain that shimmered in his eyes.

"It's nothing," he said.

She turned away with a rustle on the chair, and she stared into the dark kitchen. There, too, she thought, was the result of this so glorious party: the uneaten sandwiches, the drinks all watery with melted ice cubes, the glasses and dishes broken, the crumpled napkins smudgy with lipstick wiped from many a guilty visage.

A hardly audible chuckle sounded in her throat, a brief light of amusement took away the haggard dullness in her eyes. It never failed to amuse, if only for seconds—this spectacle of passion unleashed, snuffing about like a freed puppy, seeking out the hydrants of excitement. These parties designed and executed for the sole purpose of escape.

"What's funny?" he asked, half faithful in reaction to her smile, half-afraid that she was laughing at him.

Her eyes turned to him slowly, the light gone, the flat dispassion back.

"*You're* funny," she said.

And how did you answer that? His throat moved. His face, for one unguarded moment, flinted and was the face of a man. But there was no mind of a man behind the mask and the old will-less convolutions returned to his face.

"Why?" he asked. "Why am I funny?"

She just looked at him.

"Nothing," she said. "Forget it. Ignore it. Cancel it."

"No. I want to know." He knew very well he was punishing himself now.

"Will you go to bed?" Jane said. "Go to bed before I insult you some more."

"Seems to me you have always insulted me," he said surprised at his own mild courage.

She looked at him over the edge of her drink and he watched her thin throat move while she swallowed the drink. Those eyes, those cold blue eyes; detached, always inspecting.

"You ain't heard nothin' yet," she slurred. "Go to bed, will you?"

"I—"

"For Christ's sake, will you go to bed!"

There was almost an anguish in her voice as if in spite of her despising him, she wanted to reach out for comfort. He half started to his feet, his face lined with concern for her.

But when she saw him coming toward her she almost recoiled into the cushion of the chair.

"Don't come near me," she said, her voice thick with loathing.

His brow furrowed with lack of understanding. He stood in the middle of the room looking at her with blank eyes.

Her voice was almost hysterical. "I swear to God I'll jump off the balcony if you don't get out of here."

He stiffened momentarily.

"Now see here, Jane."

"What are you," she asked, "a whipping post? Don't you ever know when to quit?"

"Jane, I…"

"Is it possible, is it at all possible that I can make you quit?" she said, her voice a throaty insult. "Is there anything in the world I can say to make you bristle? Is there *one* insult in the whole world that will make you fight?"

"Honey, why don't you take a sedative and—"

"A sedative!"

A breathless gasp of laughter tore back her lips.

"Dear Christ, a sedative he wants me to take!" Her head shook quickly. "No, no. I'll bet there isn't. I'll bet there isn't a single insult in the world that would make you angry. I bet I could insult your whole family down to the last person and I could call you everything in the book and it wouldn't make any difference at all."

"Jane…"

"Oh—*Jesus*, will you shut up! You fool, you dolt, you ignoramus. You jerk, you—you *fat slob!*"

He recoiled under her words.

"There!" she snapped triumphantly. "Maybe I can get you to fight. You pig, you revolting mass of…"

The urge left as quickly as it had come. She sank back and the fire went out of her eyes. In an instant she had fallen into complete depression again. She reached out the glass to put it on the table beside the chair but she didn't make it and the glass went thumping to the floor. She sat there twisting on the chair.

Stan had put his drink down on the table by the couch. He was still shaking from her words, his body, throbbing with the pain of them. Without a word he stumbled past her chair and into the darkened bedroom. He sank down on his bed and his head dropped forward until his chin rested on his chest. He sat looking into the living room as Jane moved into sight and lay down on the couch. She had the bottle of whiskey with her and she took a drink from it. She was going to get drunk, he knew. She was going to drive herself into a cloud of forgetfulness.

He fell back on the pillow and lay there in the silence his eyes closed, listening to the sound of his own breathing; heavy and wheezing in the darkness. He fell into a troubled half-sleep.

He wasn't sure whether it was a dream or not. But it seemed as if he heard the doorbell ringing. The buzzing sound seemed to penetrate the thick layers of darkness. He stirred slightly on the mattress, his mouth twitching a little.

Then the cry of fright jerked him up to a sitting position, his eyes wide and staring, his heart jolting against his chest wall.

"What in God's—" he started to mutter, not even conscious of speaking.

Quickly, trembling, he dropped his legs over the edge of the bed and stood up.

"I said lock the door!" he heard someone command in the front hall.

That voice. It drove like a lance into his mind and made him shudder.

Vince.

Quickly he moved into the living room, hearing Jane say something inaudible, then Vince again.

"I'll shoot you if you don't! You think I care if I shoot you?"

With a gasp, Stan backed into the bedroom. The phone, quickly, the phone! He backed across the dark room, eyes fastened on the living room. He bumped into Jane's bed and fell onto it with a start. Hurriedly, he pushed up and moved for the phone on the bedside table. He jerked up the receiver and reached for the dial.

"Where's Stan?" Vince asked, entering the living room.

Stan's heart jolted and, with shaking fingers, he quickly put down the receiver. If Vince had a gun he mustn't be found calling for help. He knew what Vince was like. *God in heaven,* he thought, *how did he get out?*

Quickly he sank down on his bed and threw up his legs. *I'll pretend that I'm asleep,* his mind planned.

Maybe Vince won't do anything then. Maybe I'll get a chance to call the police.

"I told you he was asleep," Jane said.

Stan's legs twitched on the sheet. Maybe it was his imagination but she didn't sound afraid. She had cried out, yes, but now there was almost that sound of disinterest in her voice again.

He kept his eyes tightly shut. There was a murmur in the living room, then Vince snarling, "You fix it or I'll kill you!"

"All right, all right," she said quickly.

Stan twitched as the bedroom light was flicked on. He opened his eyes and started violently. It had been a long time since he'd seen Vince. He wasn't prepared for the gaunt wildness of his face, the madness glittering in his dark eyes.

"Vince," he said automatically. "What are you—"

"Get up," said Vince. "My arm is hurt."

Stan sat up and let his legs hang over the edge of the mattress. He saw that Vince kept his left arm stuck in the pocket of a black raincoat and he saw the strange, dark wetness of the sleeve.

Stan stood up quickly, looking at Vince, not knowing what to say or do. He saw Jane walk into the bathroom and heard her turn on the light. Then he heard her rummaging around in the medicine cabinet as his eyes moved back to Vince.

He twitched at Vince's sudden words.

"Hurry up!" There was a break in Vince's voice. He stood there weaving a little, his eyes glazed with pain and fright.

"Sit down, Vince," Stan said nervously. "Why don't—"

His voice broke off and he stood silent as Vince's eyes jerked over and peered at him. He saw Vince's teeth grit together.

"I can stand," Vince said, tensely. "Don't think I can't, either."

Stan swallowed. "Sure," he said, "sure you can stand, Vince. If you want to." He felt a tightening in his throat. He couldn't be sure how to talk to Vince. He never had been.

They stood looking at each other and, abruptly, a nervous, rasping laugh hovered in Vince's throat.

"Broke out," he said. "Guess you never thought I'd—"

He stopped and pressed his white lips together, then drew in a shaking breath.

"Hurry up!" he yelled at Jane. "I swear to God I'll shoot you if you don't!"

"I can't find any gauze," Jane answered quickly.

"In back, in back," Stan said.

He turned back to Vince again and stood there awkwardly looking at him. There was no sound but that of Jane in the bathroom. Stan's hands twitched at his sides. He put them behind his body and they bumped into the bedside table.

At the feel of the smooth wood, he remembered the gun in the drawer. He forced his lips together suddenly because he felt them begin to tremble. He mustn't act nervous. If he could only pull open the drawer and...

"H—how are you, Vince?" he asked in a hollow voice. Vince didn't answer right away. His thin throat moved convulsively as he swallowed. The heavy pistol in his hand slowly began to lower.

"She'll b—be right out," Stan said hurriedly. "She's getting it, isn't she?" His throat moved quickly. Behind him his fingers trembled on the knob of the drawer. Could he grab the pistol in time, could he fire before Vince? Questions muddled through his mind and made his hands shake more. His fingers twitched away from the knob as Vince looked at him.

Then Jane came into the bedroom carrying a box of gauze, a roll of tape and a bottle of iodine.

This isn't going to do much good," she said, "not for—"

"Never mind that," Vince said, voice shaking. "Bandage my arm. And don't try anything funny or I'll shoot you."

Stan watched the big black pistol waver with Vince's nervous movements. Now Jane was between him and Vince. Stan's hands moved back again and touched the drawer knob.

"It's going to hurt," Jane said in a flat, toneless voice. "Don't point the gun at me or it'll go off when I pull off your sleeve."

"Don't tell me what to do!"

Stan jerked spasmodically at the drawer but it still stuck.

After a moment, Vince lowered the point of the pistol. "Don't think I can't pull it up quick," he threatened.

"I don't think anything," Jane said and put her numbed fingers on the sleeve. She wondered why she didn't faint.

Stan watched with fear-stricken eyes as Jane started pulling at Vince's sleeve.

Vince started to shudder without control as the white-hot spears of pain jabbed at his arm and shoulder. He cut off one whine but a second came before he could control it. He forgot the sight of Jane's body so close to him. Everything was lost in the overwhelming pain. The room seemed to swell and contract in lurches of dark and light. *What if I black out!* his mind cried out in fear.

You'll practice till you collapse if need be!

He jerked away to escape and the coat came off. His mouth opened in a choking gasp of agony and he fell against the wall, his frail chest heaving. He felt a trickling of warm blood down his arm.

Jane had backed away and was looking at Vince, the black raincoat in her shaking hands. "You—you'd better go in and sit down," she heard herself say.

"Don't tell me—what to—do," he gasped.

He looked at Stan and saw Stan straighten up abruptly, a look of nervous fright on his face.

He grabbed at his pistol. "What are you trying to do!" he shouted furiously.

Stan shook his head quickly. "Nothing, nothing."

"Get in the other room!" Vince ordered furiously. *"Now!"*

Rigid with anguished frustration Stan moved away from the table.

Vince stood against the wall as the two of them moved past and entered the living room. He blinked his eyes and shook away the sweat dripping into them. He wanted to scream out in fury because the world was conspiring against him. No matter what he did, he was just driven further from his revenge. Damn it, why hadn't he killed Bob that day in the agency?

Before going into the living room he glanced over at the table where Stan had been. He didn't notice the slightly open drawer. His teeth gritted and he edged into the living room.

He started for the couch. "Come over here and fix my arm," he said, his voice hoarse and shaking. "Hurry up or I'll…"

He didn't finish. A cloud of blackness seemed to rush up from the floor like a great dark bird. He stumbled back with a gasp of fright and almost lost consciousness.

Then his calves bumped into the couch edge and he fell onto it. The flaring pain in his left arm drove knives of consciousness into his brain. He saw them both looking at him.

"Don't try anything!" he cried shrilly. "I swear to—!"
No!

But he couldn't stop it. He sat there with the tears rushing down his cheeks and his thin chest shaking with sobs. Through the quivering prisms of his tears he saw them standing there, watching him.

I'd never reach him in time, Stan was thinking. *He'd shoot me before I could reach him. There's no chance.*

Jane stood staring at Vince. Only slowly, was the shock departing, the sudden driving bolt of it that had struck when Vince had pointed the gun at her. But now the gun was not pointing at her. And Vince's face was the twisted, frightened face of a boy. She felt sick.

What a terrible product Vince's father had put forth into the world. What a hideous testament to his distorted ambition...to produce the mirror of himself.

She found herself remembering Saul Raden as he had been the night of Vince's debut in Carnegie Hall.

She remembered the almost hysterical ebullience of the man—the father reflecting the glory of his son. No, more than that—the father taking the credit for the glory of his son. A modern Svengali—that's what Saul Raden had been that night—gaunt and fever-charged, forgetting the past in a distended present. Repressing the knowledge that his own hands were useless twists of bone and meat that could no longer produce the surging glory of a Beethoven sonata or the polished effulgence of a Chopin waltz. Forgetting the auto accident that had caught him in the middle of his rising concert career, killed his bride and snapped the bones of his future like toothpicks, driving a wedge of madness into his brain.

She remembered that as she watched the son of Saul Raden sobbing on her couch, broken and mad. And she remembered the night she had tried to get Vince in bed with her.

Once again she was in the bedroom of Saul Raden's penthouse apartment, holding Vince's lean, hungry body against hers, both of them half clothed, her naked breasts pressing into him, the dark room swept with hot winds of forgetfulness.

Then the light had flared, blinding them. Saul Raden stood in the doorway, a supercilious twist on his lips, not the shadow of an emotion on his face. Vince started up with a gasp, his face mottled with shame. And Saul's voice fell over them like a spray of splintered ice.

"Dear boy, do go to the bathroom and wash off your face. You look positively bizarre."

She remembered the fury in her, the snapping of control. She remembered shattering the whiskey bottle over the edge of the table and lunging at Vince—knowing, even in her madness, that the only way to hurt Saul was to hurt Vince's hands.

And the whiteness, the sudden rigid pallor of Saul's face; she remembered that. Remembered his lean, white-scarred hands clamping on her wrists, the twisted wound of his mouth shouting at her, "If you dare touch his hands I swear to God I'll kill you!"

And now that son of Saul Raden was looking up at her, brushing aside tears and swallowing.

And saying in a low, throaty voice, "Bandage my arm."

She blinked and looked down at the gauze, tape, and iodine still in her hands.

Without thinking she walked to the couch and sat down beside Vince. "Put it down," she said, looking at the gun that shook in his hand. "I'm not going to take it away from you."

Vince rested the pistol in his lap. "You'd better not try," he warned. "I'll kill you if you do."

Words, words, she thought, hardly hearing what he said. She was winding gauze around his upper arm, over the wound. She didn't tear open his shirt.

"Do you want iodine on it?" she asked, suddenly conscious of the fact that Stan was standing near the bedroom door watching.

Vince's throat moved. Why did she have to ask him?

He hated to concentrate on extraneous things. He had to concentrate on one thing—making it crowd out all unimportant things. *Kill Bob, kill Bob, kill...*

"Yes," he said quickly.

"It'll hurt," she said. "A lot..."

"Then don't put it on!" he snapped in a nerve-ragged voice. "What's the matter with you?"

Jane's lips pressed together, her mind more conscious of the situation again. He's like a sullen little boy, she thought— only the little boy was wounded and he had a big gun in his hand. She wondered idly if the gun was really loaded.

Stan was standing near the bedroom door. *Could I run in, lock the door, and get the gun before he could shoot open the lock?* His throat tightened. It seemed reasonable enough. But he didn't move. He kept watching the two of them on the couch. He heard Jane say, "You'll have to go to a doctor."

Vince started to answer, then gritted his teeth in pain and anger. She was just trying to make things more complicated. She knew he couldn't go to a doctor. And he couldn't leave there because they'd call the police and the police would take him back and they'd kill him for stabbing Harry with the bottle.

Why did everyone conspire against him? Why did everything go wrong? He had to get to Bob McCall. He had to free Ruth. It was his duty.

Your duty is to the piano, Vincent, only to the piano. Saul's words again filtering through the years like a poisonous gas. Liar! He had no duty to the piano. He looked down at his arm, feeling the throbbing hot pain in it. Then, in a moment of terrible shock, he wondered if he would ever play again.

He felt his stomach tighten. *To never play again.*

The world fell on him. Visions ran through his mind—he was onstage in Carnegie Hall, one empty tuxedo sleeve in his pocket, the other hand moving futilely over the keys, trying to play both parts at once. And people in the audience, silently shaking their heads. A pity, such a pity—he might have been one of the greats.

Jane looked at him in surprise when he sobbed. There was something in her eyes he didn't want to see—something that looked too much like pity.

"Don't look at me," he gasped. "I swear to God I'll kill you if you do."

As he raised the gun to point it at her he noticed Stan moving near the bedroom door. His eyes fled over and he saw Stan's face blanch.

"What are you doing?" he asked.

"Nothing," Stan said.

"You better not try anything, Stan," Vince gasped. "I swear to God I'd just as soon…"

His throat clogged and he swallowed. He had to get rid of Stan; he didn't like Stan to stand there like that.

"Get in the kitchen," he ordered. "Make me some coffee. I want some coffee."

"All right, all right," Stan said. "I'll make some for you."

Jane heard the bare feet moving across the rug, heard Stan flicking on the kitchen light, and she silently cursed him for his cowardice. She went on bandaging.

Stan stood in the middle of the bleak kitchen looking around for a weapon. He felt his heart thudding fitfully as his eyes moved over the walls, into the partially opened cabinets, over the stove and refrigerator.

He moved to the drawer in a step. Slowly, carefully, he drew it out without making a sound. He looked down at the long, shining knives.

"What are you doing?" Vince called.

Stan twitched and hurriedly pushed in the drawer. "Making coffee!" he answered. And in his mind the accusation came. *You're afraid, you're a coward.*

In the living room, Vince was looking at the black nightgown Jane wore. As she moved her hands around his arm, tightening and pulling snug, he saw the movement of her uncupped breasts and he felt that strange, dismaying heat in his body again. It was wrong; he knew it was wrong.

The heat had come often in his young life. Saul had mocked it. Endlessly, Vince had fought that shapeless fire in his body, trying to force down the flames and, in so doing, only fanned them higher. Until they scorched.

He lowered his eyes when he saw that she noticed him staring at her breasts.

"I—I want a cigarette," he said nervously.

"Over there," Jane said, gesturing at the table beside the chair across the room.

"Get me some," Vince said.

She got up and moved over the rug. He let his eyes run up and down her body. As she stood before the table, he could see her body outlined against the lamplight. His mouth pressed together angrily.

"Bitch," he muttered, thinking she wouldn't hear.

Her mouth tightened and her throat moved as she picked up the box of cigarettes. She knew Vince was looking at her body. She wondered, momentarily, if she could use her body as a weapon.

Forcing away the tight look, she turned and brought back the cigarettes. As she lit one for him her eyes moved over his tight, boy-like face.

"How did you get out?" she asked.

"That's my business," he said, "not yours."

But, after a moment, a thin, confident smile raised his lips. The throbbing wasn't so bad, the bleeding had stopped. Why not tell her, scare her?

"I'm going to kill somebody," he said as casually as he could. He liked the sound of the words.

Her eyes were on him.

"I'm going to shoot somebody right in the head," he told her.

He didn't understand the look in her eyes. Then she bent over and it seemed that, accidentally, as she did, the nightgown fell away from her breasts. He stared with sick eyes, the hot churning starting in his stomach again.

Her eyes looked up at him now, suddenly inviting.

It worked exactly opposite. He didn't know why; she didn't know why. But, suddenly, rage exploded in his mind and he flailed out with his pistol.

His aim was poor and the barrel end raked across her right temple, tearing open the skin. Jane fell back in fright, one hand flung up to protect herself.

"Bitch!" Vince yelled at her.

Stan came in hurriedly, his face slack with fear.

"Get in and make me some coffee, I said!" Vince screamed. Stan backed away toward the kitchen, his eyes on Jane.

"Are you all right?" he asked. He waited. "Jane?" he said.

"Make coffee, make coffee," she said, her voice low and hating.

She sat there looking at Vince, her lips tight, feeling the thin dribble of blood on her temple. *I hope the police come and shoot him down like a dog. I hope they blow him to pieces.*

She saw him looking at her breasts again, and she turned away with a shudder.

Stan stood trembling before the stove, watching the coffee perk.

He started as Vince came far enough into the kitchen so he could watch both him and Jane.

"Just don't try anything," Vince said, bluffing a menace he didn't feel. "Make me a sandwich too. I'm hungry."

"A sandwich," Stan said weakly as Vince walked out of the kitchen. He opened up the drawer again and looked in at the knives. *I have to,* he thought. *I have to...*

Vince walked around the living room, ignoring Jane.

Then he stopped and looked around the room impatiently. Why was he staying here? He had to get to Bob's apartment. He had his job, his obligation to Ruth.

But *how!* How did he get to Bob's apartment without Stan and Jane warning the police?

I'll rip out the phone, he thought. He was suddenly pleased at the invention of his mind.

But the smile faded. They could go out after he left, call from a neighbor's phone or from a phone booth in some store. And he couldn't afford to waste two bullets. He might not even have them.

He fumbled with the gun, trying to open it so he could see how many bullets there were. But he knew nothing of guns and he couldn't get it open. A hiss of anger passed his lips.

Then he found his eyes suddenly on the telephone beside the chair he was in. He looked at the black receiver and at the dial.

And the smile returned.

3:15 a.m.

He grunted a little and felt Ruth's legs twitch against him. Then he cleared his throat and tried to go back to sleep but the jangling wouldn't let him.

He felt her hand on his shoulder.

"Honey?" she whispered.

He woke up. "Uh?"

"Telephone."

"Oh, my God," he muttered disgustedly.

He pulled back the covers and let his legs down to the floor. As he stood he winced at the cold of the floorboards against his feet.

"Who could it be?" he heard her murmur from the dark warmth of the bed.

"God knows," he said, yawning, and walked around the edge of the bed. In the living room the phone kept ringing.

"All right, all right," he mumbled.

He picked up the receiver with sleep-numbed fingers.

"Yeah," he said.

"*Bob.*"

Just his name; but the way it was spoken shook away the mists around his brain.

"Yes," he answered.

"This is Stan, Bob. I—could you come over?"

"What?" Bob's voice rose in unpleasant surprise.

"Could you—Bob, could you come over?" Stan's voice was tightly urgent.

Bob yawned. "What time is it?" he asked.

"I..." There was a pause. "About three fifteen."

"My God, what are you doing, having a party?" Bob asked.

There was another pause.

"No, no—the party is over."

And the way Stan said that. It made Bob shudder; and, suddenly awake, he thought, *My God, he's killed Jane!*

His throat moved.

"You want me to come over?" he asked, not knowing what to say.

"Y-yes, Bob. Can you?"

"I guess so." He took a deep breath. "All right, Stan, I'll be right over," he said. "Are you...?"

The receiver dropped abruptly on the other end of the line and Bob stood there a moment in the darkness holding the receiver to his ear. Then, slowly, he put down the receiver and went back into the bedroom.

"Who was it?" Ruth asked.

"Stan."

"Stan? Why did he call?"

"I don't know, hon. He wants me to come over."

"Now?"

"Yes. I think I'd better go, too."

Silence a moment; she felt her heartbeat quicken.

"All right if I turn on the light?" he asked.

"Yes, of course, honey." Her voice was soft and concerned.

He turned on the bedside lamp and saw her propped up on one elbow looking at him. As the lamp flared on she blinked and closed her eyes a moment. Then she opened them and looked back at him.

"What's wrong, Bob?"

"He didn't say, honey," he told her. "He just wanted me to come over."

"Did he sound upset?"

He started taking off his pajamas.

"Yes," he said, "he did."

She caught her breath.

"Jane," she said quickly.

He swallowed, then nodded his head.

"That's what I was thinking," he said.

"Oh, *no,*" she said. "It couldn't be. He *loves* her."

"How much can a guy take?" was his answer.

Quickly he dressed and she watched him pull on his trousers and tuck in the shirt ends with quick movements.

"Shall I go with you?" she asked.

"No, honey," he said. "Stay in bed; you need your rest. And—" he blew out a breath, "if it's what we think, I'd rather you weren't there to see it."

He sat down on the bed and started pulling on his socks.

"I wonder why he called us," he said.

"Maybe he didn't know whom to call."

"Poor guy," he said. "All those people who come to his parties—and probably not one of them he could call his friend."

She shook her head.

"I hope it's not what we think," she said.

"You probably think it's a ruse of Jane's to get me over there," he said.

He saw from the way her eyes lowered that he'd guessed right.

"Lie down, dumkopf," he murmured and pushed her head down on the pillow with a gentle movement.

"Will you be gone long?" she asked.

"I don't know, honey. I guess, if it's what we think, it'll just be a matter of calling the police."

He looked at her for a moment. Then he pressed her back again on the pillow and kissed her warm mouth.

"Go to sleep," he said.

"Don't stay too long," she said. "I'll worry."

"I won't," he promised. "I—well, I just hope we *are* wrong and it's something else."

"Oh, so do I."

He kissed her again and stood up. Reaching down he turned out the lamp.

She lay in the silence of the bedroom listening to his footsteps move across the living room and stop at the hall closet. She heard the hangers rattle as he took his jacket out, then the front door shut quietly and she was alone in the apartment.

She looked at the radium-dialed clock and saw that it was almost three-thirty.

She made a worried sound in her throat. Was it really what Bob thought? Had Stan finally lost his mind and done it? She rustled her head on the pillow. Not that she could blame Stan. Even if Jane was her friend, she knew as well as anyone that she had been no wife to Stan, that she kept Stan at a peak of nerves with her parties and her drive and her ceaseless, open infidelities.

And Stan was the type that would take it and take it, quietly, without a scene or a complaint until, one day, one night, he would snap right down the middle, rise up and slay. It was something she and Bob had discussed often. Bob had always predicted it would end like this.

She lay there quietly and then, abruptly, she was sitting up and staring into the darkness.

Was it that? Had Stan killed her? Suddenly, and for no apparent reason, she felt her heart begin to beat in great, anxious pulses and felt her hands trembling on the sheet.

Bob had joked with her about it and she had smiled; but was it so incredible that Jane might have called and asked him over? No, no, no, how could she believe that? Would Bob lie to her and tell her that Stan had phoned if it were Jane?

And yet, she couldn't stop the heavy heartbeats; she couldn't check her trembling hands. Her breath quickened. She knew what Jane was like. She had seen the savage lusts she could arouse in herself at the slightest notice, knew she had no discretion at all when it came. And she knew she loved Bob too much. She loved him so much that trusting him wasn't enough. She didn't trust another woman in the world.

She shook her head, furious at herself. This is ridiculous, she thought. *I'm going crazy. I'm making up everything. He's gone to Stan's apartment because Stan asked him to.*

But *why* did Stan ask him to?

She felt caught up in It horrible vortex whose inner currents would not let her loose. Suddenly, from nothing, she had built up a monster of suspicions and fears. Was this the lot of the pregnant woman? No, she thought, she was just a suspicious woman. She was too possessive and possessiveness bred suspicions.

She closed her eyes. She must go to sleep and wait for him to come back. She must believe in her husband.

But she found herself reaching and turning on the lamp. She found herself standing on the cold floor, shivering. *And now what*, she asked herself, *what do you intend to do; run after him?*

Horribly enough, that was exactly what she wanted to do.

She almost cried aloud, so miserable did it make her that doubt persisted despite all reason. Not doubt, really, she tried to amend in her own favor; not doubt, but fear. She was afraid for Bob, so terribly afraid for him. She shuddered.

What if there was something else entirely? What if Jane had told Stan she had slept with Bob? What if, drunk and mean, she had taunted Stan until the breaking point had come? What if, striking out blindly, she had accused Bob too, hoping to wound Stan by firing a buckshot charge of unfaithfulness at him, a charge that included every man she knew? Ruth knew how nasty and horrible Jane could get, how she'd say anything to hurt somebody she disliked.

She couldn't sleep now. She hurried nervously to the bureau and pulled clothes from her drawer. She didn't care what the reason was, she didn't care if Bob wanted her to stay home, she had to find out why Stan had called.

The nightgown rustled to the floor and her body broke out in tiny goose bumps as the cold air covered her.

Ten minutes later she had phoned for a cab, dressed and was moving down the stairs quickly.

3:20 a.m.

After he put down the phone, Stan turned away, unable to look at Jane. He felt his hands trembling at his sides.

"How *brave*," she said, "leading him here to be killed. Your own friend."

"What did you want me to do?" he muttered, sick with shame.

"Why don't you—" she started.

"Shut up, both of you," Vince said calmly.

Vince felt peace now. He felt very pleased with himself. He'd done something very clever. He had circumvented time and space. He didn't have to leave now, didn't have to worry about Stan and Jane calling the police. He didn't have to go after his prey. His prey was coming to him.

Satisfied, very confident, and pleased, he walked over and sat on the piano bench. He sat there looking at Jane on the couch in her almost transparent nightgown, then over at Stan who was looking out the window, his body looking heavy and ridiculous in those stupid pajamas.

Spritely music tinkled in Vince's mind—Liadov's *Music Box* coupled with a Chopin *Valse Brilliante*—a dissonant but sparklingly exciting tonal companionship.

Now it was just a matter of waiting. Everything was going right for a change. His arm still hurt, but the fiery, stabbing pain was gone. It had lessened to a dull, gnawing ache. He could stand that. He could stand a lot of things, as long as he knew that Bob was coming.

He held the pistol in his lap and looked at it. He tried to open it again. But there was only one hand available and his teeth gritted in irritation when the gun wouldn't open.

Stan stood looking over the sleeping city. His eyes were bleak and his body felt tight, constrained within binds of shame and aching fear. He knew he shouldn't have called Bob. He should have refused. Now it was too late. Bob was on his way. His body was tense with the knowledge.

And now he was an absolute coward in Jane's eyes. That was the worst element of it. His eyes closed slowly and his chest shuddered with a convulsive breath. He had to do something. He had to get the gun away from Vince. Before Bob got there.

"I'd like to get a robe," he heard Jane say then and he looked over his shoulder. "It's cold in here," she told Vince.

Vince looked at her. He didn't want her to put on the robe. He wanted to look at her like this. It added something to the scene. It was like an exciting moment in a thriller movie and he liked the feeling it gave him.

He felt very sure of himself as he stood and walked slowly to the wall thermostat, always watching them from the corners of his eyes.

He moved the tiny, serrated wheel until the dial rested at seventy-five degrees. Then he looked over at Jane.

"There," he said. "No need to be cold. Don't bother to put on a robe now. You don't need a robe."

He felt his throat contract at the look in her eyes. He forced a smile to his lips to hide the nervousness.

"What would you do if I didn't have this gun?" he said. He felt like exchanging sharp, bitter dialogue. It was exciting now. He told himself that. Exciting and invigorating. Everything going according to plan. He was in complete charge of the moment, master of the situation. He had beaten everyone—Harry and the guard and that girl and the man in the subway—everyone. They had all tried to keep him from his purpose, but he had beaten them. And now he had Jane and Stan at bay, too, and he was going to have Bob in his hands soon. Yes, everything was fine.

"What would you do?" he said again, shaking slightly.

She turned her head away and rubbed her white forearms with her palms. Vince swallowed. "I asked you a question," he said.

She heard the words before she knew she'd said them. "Oh, go to hell."

She didn't notice how Stan turned, his face tightened into a mask of fright. She felt only incredible wonder at herself.

Vince had stiffened, his hand tightening on the revolver.

"Maybe I'll kill you," he said, trying desperately to frighten her.

"Maybe you will," she said and, even as she said it, felt her stomach turning over. *I must be crazy.*

Vince turned away from her suddenly. She was trying to trick him into wasting his bullets. Well, he wouldn't waste any, he told himself and his finger twitched away from the trigger. She wasn't worth a bullet. Not yet.

Women are expendables, Vincent, women are trying bitches.

He nodded to himself, driving confidence back. Yes, if there were any bullets left after he'd killed Bob then Jane would be the one to get them. Right in her chest. He got a pleasant distracting sense of warmth in his body at the thought of firing right into those arching breasts.

He sat down and looked at her. After a moment he looked at the floor. Why did Bob take so long? Vince took a nervous breath. He had to come soon. They might find the guard, they might find Harry. The girl might go to the police. His lips started to shake a little. No, no, don't get upset, he told himself anxiously. *It's going to be all right, all right.*

He sat there looking at something red under his nails.

Stan stood by the chair looking at Jane, then at Vince. He had to do something. He couldn't leave that look in Jane's eyes. Even if he died for it, he had to take that look from her eyes.

But what was there to do?

Vince's hands twitched in his lap. He heard a clock ticking in the kitchen. He *should* have done something to that girl, he thought. He could have, too; you bet your life he could have—she was that kind of girl. You could tell by looking at them. Filthy. Something about the way they talk and dress. Like Jane—sure. Jane was one of them too. He'd like to—

No. He held himself tensely. That was wrong, it was dirty.

"What time is it?" he suddenly asked.

Stan raised his arm nervously and looked at his watch. "Twenty-five to four," he said.

"Good," Vince said, "that's just what I want."

He didn't know what he meant by that but he liked the sound of the words. It sounded as if he had planned everything to the last detail and it was all working out perfectly. He smiled to himself and brushed back his thick hair with a casual movement of his right hand. As he did, the gun thumped down on the floor.

Stan started forward, then jerked to a stop as Vince pulled up the gun and pointed it at him.

"You wanna die?" he asked Stan, eyes glittering. "Do you?"

Stan's throat moved and he started to shake his head, then stopped.

Jane pushed up abruptly and started toward the bedroom. "I'm going to get my robe," she said.

Stan's heart leaped and he felt his body tensing. "Jane..."

Vince watched her moving and felt heat begin to churn up in his stomach. She couldn't do that to him! Bitch! He stood up in a quick movement, feeling his left arm start to throb. No, no, you have to save the bullets.

"You'd better watch out," he said.

"Jane, stay away from the—*phone*," Stan said suddenly. He'd meant to say *gun* but then he decided there might still be a chance for him to get it, and he changed it to *phone*. All he wanted to do was alert Vince anyway so she wouldn't try anything.

Jane had stopped and was looking at Stan with hate in her eyes.

"You *fool*," she said bitterly.

Stan stood there helplessly, feeling a terrible heaviness in his stomach.

Vince pushed Jane aside now, his fingers twitching as he touched the smoothness of the gown over her warm hip. Then he turned on the bedroom light and his eyes moved around.

"Going to try something funny, haah?" he said.

"She wasn't going to try anything," Stan heard himself saying loudly. "Don't do anything to her. Vince, I'm begging you."

"Oh, shut up!" Jane snapped, her nerves frayed. "Haven't you got a scrap of man in you?"

Stan pressed his lips together stubbornly. "I don't want anything to happen to you," he said.

For a long moment they looked at each other while they heard Vince tearing out phone wires.

"Something has happened to me," Jane said in a low, trembling voice. "I know this is the end. I know I'm married to a—a—"

She turned away and brushed past Vince.

Vince stood watching her as she put on her robe. His throat moved as the backward movement of her shoulders made her taut breasts press against the silk. His tongue ran nervously over his upper lip, licking at the tiny sweat drops. No, he heard the voice in his mind, *no, that's dirty.*

"All right," he said, forcing the swagger back into his voice. "Now get in the living room or I'll shoot you."

Trembling, she walked past him. She moved to the bar and reached for the whiskey bottle. Bob was coming over. The thought made her stomach fall. It would kill Ruth if anything happened to Bob. Especially now. Her throat tightened. It mustn't happen. It *mustn't*.

"Make me a drink, too," Vince said slyly.

At first she tightened and was going to tell him to make his own. Then she remembered the night in the bedroom with Vince. Vince could never have done those things sober. Maybe drink plus her body could get the gun away from him.

She hid the whiskey bottle from Vince so he wouldn't see how much of it she poured in and how little soda after it. When she turned, he was sitting on the piano bench. She walked over and held out the glass to him. She made a point of taking a slow, deep breath as she stood before him. Her bosom rose and pressed against the dark silk.

"There," she said, trying hard to keep the hatred from her voice.

Vince reached out casually, holding the gun and then, with a downward snap of the barrel, he smashed the glass in her hand. She recoiled at the pain of the glass splinters lancing into her palm, and streaks of red drove up her cheeks.

"*You*—"

Vince shoved the barrel against her chest and pushed her away from him.

"Vince, don't!" he heard Stan cry out in an agonized voice. He saw Stan move quickly to Jane and try to put his arms around her. She tore loose with a wracking sob and stumbled back to the couch, looking down at her cut palm.

"You stay away from her!" Vince ordered, and Stan backed away, face torn with conflicting emotions.

Vince looked at Jane then and smiled bitterly. "You think I'd drink that crap?" he said, voice sneering. "You think I'm dumb? Well, *you're* dumb."

She sat there trembling. And, within her taut fury, she felt something else—*alarm*. Vince was clever. Simple expedients would not topple his craftiness.

She wiped her hand on a cushion, teeth gritted. Her brow furrowed. Where was Bob now? If he took his car he'd almost be there. From 18th Street to 54th Street wasn't even two miles. And in the early morning streets there would be no traffic to contend with.

Oh, God, let him have the flat tire of his life! she prayed.

Stan was in the chair now looking over at his wife. Deep in his vitals he felt the body-wrenching shame her scorn had lashed into him. It was worse than before. Then, at least, she'd been talking of things he could accept—her unfaithfulness, her restless dissatisfaction. He allowed those things and wanted her anyway.

There were excuses for almost everything, if you looked hard enough for them. But for outright cowardice there was none. He felt his muscles tightening, feeling more than sickness now. He felt drained.

"You still managing?" he heard Vince say.

He looked up blankly. "What?"

"You still a concert manager?" Vince asked again.

For a moment Stan looked at him blankly, afraid that Vince was trying to trap him into something.

"Yes," he said. "I am."

A shaky smile flitted across Vince's lips. "You still got Dinotti?"

"Dinotti?"

"You still *manage* him?" Vince's voice was rising.

"I...yes," Stan nodded. "Dinotti's still with me." What was Vince driving at? It made Stan nervous to figure it.

"How *are* things?" Vince asked.

Stan didn't know what to make of the question. Here Vince was planning to kill Bob and yet he was asking casual questions about the concert field. It was ghoulish.

"It's all right, I guess," he answered nervously.

He glanced over at Jane but she was leaning back on the couch, her head fallen forward in mute dejection.

Vince felt his hands start to tremble. He knew he shouldn't be asking. It was crazy to ask and, anyway, what did the concert field matter to him? But...

"Got many *pianists?*" he asked in a timorous voice, as a child might ask a candy storeowner if he had any chocolates to spare.

Stan suddenly realized he was trying to get him to manage him again! He *was* insane.

Abruptly, the idea came.

"Not too many," he said, acting on it impulsively. "Not of your stature, anyway."

He felt his heart begin to beat heavily. Could Vince hear the lie? He closed his hands into white fists on his knees.

Vince couldn't tell it was a lie. An anxious, half-eager smile raised his thin lips, then was gone nervously. Blood pulsed through his body making his arm ache. That wouldn't matter, he assured himself quickly. A bullet can be taken out, there's nothing fatal about a bullet in your arm.

"Would you like to get back into the—the field?" Stan asked.

Oh, God, it was such an errant lie. How could Vince possibly swallow it? He had killed, he had escaped from an insane asylum and now he was being asked to believe it was possible for him to return to concert work.

But he didn't know how anxious Vince was, he didn't know that Vince wanted more than anything else in the world to believe just that.

"Well..." Vince's voice hesitated. He had to catch himself. He mustn't be too eager. The thought came warning, cautioning.

Jane was looking up at Stan now.

"There's a need, a very great need for good pianists," Stan was saying, fists trembling in his lap. "The field is shallow. Very shallow."

"But my—my *arm*," Vince said, tense at the confession.

Stan's throat moved quickly, he strained forward in the chair.

"Your arm can be fixed," he said.

"You think so?" Voice shakingly eager.

"Of course, of course it can," Stan went on, afraid lest the assurance slip from his voice and unmask his stratagem. "Look at Dinotti. A broken wrist—and him a violinist. Is he any the worse for it?"

That was true. Vince knew that. Dinotti had been out on Long Island Sound in a sailboat and the swinging boom had broken his wrist. Now he was as good as ever. And his arm could be fixed too. Blood flowed faster in his veins as his heartbeat quickened. To play again, to really play.

"You really think so?" he asked, anxious to have Stan tell him the same thing again.

"I do," Stan said. "I'm sure of it." He felt his confidence growing. Vince was only an impressionable boy.

Now Jane's heart was beating quickly too as she looked over at Vince. Maybe Stan had some redeeming feature after all. If not courage then craft. It was better than nothing. Jane leaned forward on the couch.

"You want me to play?" Vince suddenly blurted out. And a hot flush crossed his face. He shouldn't have said that. But he wanted so to play, to be told he was good enough for concert work again. All right, he hated Saul; he'd hated what Saul did to him. But, in spite of every torturing hour of practice, he loved the piano.

Stan was sweating now. He felt large drops of it trickling down across his chest. He thought of the way Vince had looked at the piano before. A look of adoration, of hungry longing.

Was it possible that he could get the gun from Vince?

Maybe he could undo his failure and save Bob after all. A flood of hope covered him. He was excited and eager to save Bob, to gain Jane's respect. It could all come back in a rush. Jane would love him again, everything would be wonderful again. Swelling imagination filled him.

"Sure," he said eagerly. "Sure, Vince, play someth—"

His voice suddenly broke off and sweat broke out faster on him. *If he uses his left hand he'll know he can't play, he'll know I'm lying.* Stan raised his left hand and wiped it across his mouth nervously.

"Why don't we talk terms first?" he said awkwardly. "We could..."

"What shall I play?" Vince asked eagerly.

Like a little boy, he was now eager to do right. Quickly, getting rid of it, he put the gun on top of the piano. He wanted to play, to have Stan take out contracts and maps, plan a season for him. His hands shook at the thought.

Jane was tensing herself on the couch. How fast could she get to the piano and grab the gun?

"Well, why don't we—?" Stan started.

"Shall I play the Polonaise?" Vince asked, forgetting about his left hand completely.

Stan swallowed hard. "No, no," he said hastily, then forced a smile to his lips as Vince looked suspicious. "I mean," he went on quickly, "you're out of practice, Vince. You should start out easy. You know that."

"What shall I play, then?" Vince asked sullenly.

Stan glanced at the piano, at the gun resting on top. He forced his eyes back to Vince. If he could get Vince so distracted with playing that he could get the gun...

"Well, I don't know," he fumbled for time. "You have to remember it's going to be a little rough but—"

His voice broke off as Vince looked at him coldly.

"Well, you know you haven't played in a long time," he said, new sweat breaking out on his face and body.

"I'm as good as ever," Vince said in a tight, hard voice. "I can play better than anybody."

"You bet you can, Vince," Stan said. "Sure. I just—"

Good God, how did you reason with a lunatic? His mind raced and tripped over itself, trying to find a piece that had no left hand.

"I said what shall I play?" Vince said, losing patience.

"How about—Chabig's *Tantivy?*" Stan lunged for a suggestion. *The left hand doesn't come in for at least twenty measures,* he exulted inwardly.

"Oh, all right," Vince said.

Jane's eyes were fastened on the heavy pistol on the piano. When Vince got into the piece she'd try for it.

Stan was sweating again. The piece was fast, very fast. What if even Vince's *right* hand wasn't as good as it had been? What if he made mistakes and faltered, lost his temper? He dug nails fiercely into his palms. *He's got to be able to play it, he's got to...*

Vince turned from them, a smile faltering on his lips.

Yes, that was a good one. He thought of the long hours of practice he'd spent memorizing this piece. In his mind, he saw the score as clearly as if the music were resting on the piano.

His right hand arched over the keys, settling like a diffident spider. The pads of his fingertips pressed into the ivory keys to get the feel of them. From the corner of his eyes he saw Stan get up. It didn't matter. He could get the gun before they could do anything.

He looked back at the keyboard, hearing the flurry of Saul's old commands like cool winds in his mind. *Never drive down the keys, never use your fingers like senseless mallets. Press. Make the note ring clear and certain. Combine. Blend. Build to the climax.*

In the quiet of the room the first notes of the *Tantivy* sprinkled.

Jane slid to the edge of the couch with a careful, guarded movement. Stan saw her move and caught his breath. He suddenly realized she was going to try for the gun and he almost started running for the piano.

He caught himself. He took a slow, wary step toward the piano. It seemed as if he hardly moved at all.

The music sprayed through the room, an icy clatter of notes. No fear of his right hand, Stan noted with the back of thought. Vince's touch was, as ever, supreme. He took another step, feeling his throat tighten.

The gypsy violence discorded into his ears as he edged closer. Surely Vince could see him coming. But Vince was absorbed in his playing. Stan tightened as he saw Vince's left hand slowly raising and preparing to strike. Chabig had saved the left hand in order to make the entry one of shocking dissonance. The pianist struck with all his power a chord of five notes. Stan moved more quickly, his hands shaking. What if Vince saw him coming?

Now Jane looked up and saw Stan coming closer. But she knew the piece too and knew that any second Vince's left hand would smash down on the keys.

She stood up. She was almost behind Vince and he couldn't see her clearly. Stan couldn't get there in time; she had to get the gun.

Stan tried to catch her eye, but her attention had returned to the piano and the heavy black pistol on it. Stan stopped and began to shake. He hadn't meant it to be this way. She'd be killed!

He strained forward and was in the middle of a step as Vince's left hand drove down on the keys.

The gagging scream of agony stiffened them both. They stood there gaping at Vince as he raised his left hand in front of his eyes.

It won't play! The words were like a hot flame playing on his brain. He tried to move the fingers but they were like rotted sausages. And a shooting pain filled his arm.

His face grew taut, the vein at his right temple began to throb, and suddenly, with a wrenching sob, he drove his clenched left hand down on the keys. He jerked up the bunched hand and drove it down again, smashing down a cluster of white and black keys, filling the room with thick dissonance.

Jane broke into a run for the piano.

Stan couldn't hold back the cry. *"Jane!"*

Vince leaped up at the yell and knocked back the piano bench. As he lunged for the pistol, Jane jumped on him and they both went crashing into the piano.

Stan started forward, eyes widening, hands snapping into fists.

Vince screamed into Jane's face as she drove a fist into his wounded arm. He jerked up the pistol but she shoved it aside and he couldn't get a grip on the trigger.

She struck at him again, but missed and lost her balance. Vince felt her soft body against him. From the corner of his eye he saw Stan rushing at him.

With a strangled cry he ripped the gun up and drove it across her temple. Jane reeled back with a dull cry and fell on her back.

Stan jolted back as the gun was shoved out at him. He stepped back and almost tripped.

Vince stood there breathing hoarsely.

"Trick me, haah?" he gasped.

He turned toward Jane who lay motionless on the floor. Slowly he turned the pistol on her.

"I'm going to blow your guts out," he said in a low, choked voice.

Then, suddenly, his breath stopped. He stood there, stomach and chest trembling while his eyes focused on the hallway that led to the front door.

The doorbell was ringing.

3:40 a.m.

The cab pulled up to the curb and Ruth got in quickly.

"367 West 54th," she told the driver.

"Yes, ma'am."

The driver pulled the door shut and the cab pulled away from the curb. The street was completely silent except for the sound of the motor.

Ruth shivered as she settled back on the cold leather seat. *I hope he isn't angry when he sees me,* she thought. *What if he knows what I'm thinking; about Jane trying to get him there?*

Her throat moved. Maybe she should go home. Maybe it would be better. Nothing could be wrong. Maybe it was better she just went home to bed and let herself worry. That was better than Bob's knowing she hadn't trusted him.

But it wasn't a matter of trust, she told herself.

Oh, it was no use arguing with herself. She might as well clear her mind of everything. She was going and that was all there was to it. She loved him too much to lie awake at home, tossing on the bed and dying a thousand deaths of fear each second. It was no use. If she was going to make a faux pas, then she was going to make it. Better than a nervous breakdown of concern.

Bob would forgive her when he knew she only did it because she was afraid.

The cab crossed Twenty-Second and, at Twenty-Third, turned right and headed toward Lexington.

"Could you go a little faster," she asked.

"Beg pardon, ma'am?"

"Could—could you drive a little faster. This is rather urgent."

"Yes, ma'am."

Rather urgent. Now she really felt silly. She could just visualize all of them together and the cab driver telling them, *So she tells me to drive faster, see?* And then they'd all break into breathless laughter.

She almost smiled at herself, the scene seemed so real.

But what if it were true? What if Bob was in danger?

Time suddenly fell on her like a weight. How far had he gone? Was he at Stan's apartment yet? She'd had to dress, go downstairs, and wait for the cab.

She leaned forward.

"I'm sorry to bother you but—do you have the time?"

"Quarter to four, ma'am," the driver said.

"Thank you."

"Be there in a jiffy, ma'am."

She smiled as she leaned back on the cold seat.

It was that tightness in her stomach she couldn't rid herself of. It wasn't intuition, she knew that. This business about pregnant woman's intuition was just a lark she'd made up for Bob. No, she was worried, that was all. She couldn't help it.

Anyway, she rationalized, how would any woman feel to have her husband called away at almost four o'clock in the morning? How would any woman like to be wrenched from sleep, and watch her husband dress and leave her? Especially when she wasn't sure why he was going, even where he was going. No, pregnancy had nothing to do with it. Any sensitive woman would worry under circumstances like that.

She took a nervous breath of the cold morning air. Why did it have to happen? She felt such a horrible foreboding. It was probably just because it had happened in the dead of the night. It was a strange time, a silent, barren time. It was a frightening time, this lonely empty shell of hours that was not night and not day. And it frightened her to be out in the streets in a cab now.

Up Lexington Avenue, past the silent store fronts, the dead faces of the restaurants, now and then past the thin, green neon of a bar still open, people in there drinking. How could they be awake and living at this hour? Maybe they were another race that lives when all of us go to sleep.

Then she suddenly thought, what if she got sick to her stomach? She'd had a rough time the past few weeks. But she'd really feel foolish if she came to Stan's place and had to run right to the bathroom. A sort of harried smile crossed her lips. What would Bob say?

No more thought, she told herself. *I'm going and that's all there is to it. No matter what he says. If he yells at me I won't mind as long as it's a nice, healthy, unharmed yell. If he takes me over his knee and spanks me I won't care. As long as the hand that spanks is nice and safe and mine.*

In the darkness, in the silence of the great city, the cab sped up Lexington Avenue, its motor humming. Thirty-fifth Street, Thirty-sixth Street, Thirty-seventh, Thirty...

4:00 a.m.

Vince stiffened at the sound of the bell. The apartment seemed to shake with the sound. He stood tensely, his chest rising and falling with heavy breaths, his throat congested. He coughed. He didn't know what to do exactly.

He looked at Stan.

"All right," he said hoarsely, "you're going to—"

"Vince, for God's sake, don't do it!" Stan suddenly burst out, "He hasn't done anything to you."

Vince was going to shout at him to shut up, but he held it in. His dark eyes glittered as he spoke quickly, gutturally.

"Shut up," he said. "You're going to open the door and let him in."

Stan looked at him with blank eyes. He glanced toward Jane. His heart was thudding rapidly.

"Get out there," Vince said.

"Vince..."

Vince raised the gun and pointed it at Stan. "You want to die?"

Stan braced himself. *I'll let him shoot me,* he suddenly thought. It would warn Bob. He felt himself shudder. *No, no,* his mind rationalized quickly. *He'll shoot Jane then. You can't do it.*

But, deep inside, he knew he was a coward and afraid to die.

Vince moved behind Stan. He prodded the gun into Stan's back as Stan stopped by his wife.

Stan jolted nervously as the gun barrel touched him. He looked into the hall with sick eyes and started walking toward the door. *God, why am I doing what he tells me to?* His teeth ground together in impotent fury.

The doorbell rang again and kept on ringing. Vince felt a wild, surging elation. Now he was going to avenge Ruth. All right, he couldn't play the piano but at least he could save Ruth. He *would* save her.

Strangely enough though he couldn't feel much about Ruth. He knew he wanted revenge. But he didn't realize it wasn't Ruth he wanted to avenge. It was himself, on the world. The world that had crippled his left arm and made it impossible for him to play anymore.

They stopped.

"Now," Vince said in a grating voice, *"open the door."*

No. No, Stan tried to turn the world into sound. His fingers curled around the doorknob. Bob was his friend and yet he had brought Bob here to die. Scream out and beat on the door and warn Bob. Turn and fight Vince until the bullets were all gone from the gun into his body. He wanted to fight for Jane.

But he couldn't. He stood there, shaking and helpless, his stomach a hot, churning knot of pain. And the words stabbed at his brain drawing the blood of his self-respect, the last few drops of it. I am a coward.

"Open it!"

The cloud of Vince's hot, furied whisper surrounded him.

He unlocked the door and opened it.

"Stan, what is it?"

Bob stood in the doorway looking at Stan, white and trembling.

He moved forward.

"Stan, what—"

Then, suddenly, he leaped to the side with a gasp as the door was slammed shut from behind and he saw Vince's glaring face before him.

Stan backed away, shuddering, his eyes wide and staring. Vince leaned against the door, his chattering teeth jammed together, the gun wavering in his hand.

"Vince," was all Bob could say as he stood there, paralyzed with sudden fear.

"Get inside," Vince said.

He forced a calmness through himself. Bob was here now, in his hands. There was no use ending it right away. Bob would pay; but slowly.

"Vince, you—"

"I said get inside!" Vince ordered, his thin voice ringing out shrilly in the hallway.

Bob backed into Stan as he retreated.

"Bob, I'm sorry," Stan murmured in a weak voice. "Please don't hold it against—"

"If you don't get in there," Vince's voice was low and menacing, "I swear to God I'll..."

They backed into the living room, their eyes never leaving Vince's white, twisted face.

As they entered the living room Stan heard a groan and, turning suddenly, he saw Jane sitting up, holding her forehead with her hand, blood trickling between her white fingers.

"Jane," he muttered, brokenly.

"Leave her alone," Vince said.

But, for some reason, Stan didn't listen. Maybe it was because he felt dead already. He helped his wife up.

"Let go of me," she muttered hoarsely, in a voice that bordered on hysteria. "I don't want—"

"Be quiet," he said, quietly firm. "You haven't helped any either."

Jane sank down on the couch, wordless. She looked at Bob, then at Vince. Her teeth dug into her lower lip.

"I'm going to wash off her forehead," she heard Stan say to Vince.

Vince said nothing. He backed over to where he could watch Stan in the kitchen. Stan might try for a knife. He kept looking from Stan to Bob, the gun held tightly in his hand. *Why didn't I stop Stan from going in there?* he wondered. And then he realized that he was afraid of Stan. You couldn't trust Stan's kind, they were unpredictable. One minute they would be blubbering for pity, the next minute they would come lunging at you, eagle-clawed eyes like fire. He had seen that at the asylum. The little man who coughed, he was like that. Cry, cry, cry and then, suddenly, with a shriek and a gibber, he would leap at you.

Bob stood in the middle of the room looking first at Jane, then at Vince.

"How did you get out?" he asked weakly.

"Never mind that," Vince said carefully; "Do you want to know *why* I came out?"

Bob stared at him, his throat moving, still numbed from the shock of seeing Vince.

"I came to kill you," Vince said.

Bob started as if someone had kicked him in the stomach. He stood there, his face petrified. Vince liked that. It gave him confidence again, confidence that he'd been losing when first Jane, then Stan, had defied him. He needed constant obedience to his words or he became unnerved.

"Ki—" Bob's voice broke off. He drew in a harsh breath.

"Kill?" he said, his voice flat and unbelieving.

"I'm going to blow your brains out," Vince said, his voice a low, throaty sound. His eyes were like glowing coals.

"But—but I haven't done anything to—"

"Shut up!"

A bubbling chuckle filled Vince's throat and his nostrils flared in scorn.

"Yellow," he said. "You're afraid to die, aren't you?"

Bob's throat moved convulsively.

"Aren't you!"

"Vince, don't be crazy," Bob heard himself saying. "You don't want to kill anyone. You know you—"

Vince's laughter stopped him, made him shudder. "I don't want to kill anyone," Vince mocked. Then his face flinted. "I've killed two men to get to you. Do you really think I'm not going to..."

He broke off suddenly and almost jerked the trigger. He wanted desperately to pull the trigger and watch Bob crumple to the floor in a hail of bullets. He wanted to stand over Bob's twitching body emptying the gun into him.

The holding back made him shudder.

No, he told himself. *Wait; enjoy yourself.* He wondered briefly if he should make Bob call up Ruth and get her over here too. How she would love him if she saw him shoot Bob right before her eyes. Then she'd give herself to him right in front of Stan and Jane.

No. No. He shouldn't think of Ruth that way. She was clean and beautiful. He wasn't insane. That proved it.

"Sit down," he told Bob.

Good. Now he was in control of himself.

Bob stared at Vince without moving. *Kill me?* The words drummed in his mind and made him shiver convulsively. He couldn't conceive of it. To suddenly have death facing you; that was impossible to understand.

"Are you going to sit down or...?"

Bob sank down on the piano bench with a faltering of leg muscles. He sat there, eyes fastened to Vince's face.

"Get out here," Vince told Stan.

He backed into the wall as Stan passed. Then he shoved Stan's back and almost made him fall over.

"Watch where you're going, stupid," he said.

Stan's breath caught and a strange, unfamiliar fury burst in him. That they should be subject to the whims of this, adolescent lunatic! It made him shake with anger.

Then, as he walked past Bob, for a moment their eyes met. And there was something in Bob's eyes that made Stan's lips tighten, that made him turn away his gaze.

"Stan," Bob said and it was like a knife turning in Stan's body.

"You're going to die, you know that," Vince said.

He wanted to frighten Bob more. He liked the look Bob had gotten in the hall; that drained, terrified look, one cheek twitching; the backing away in horror. Vince liked that a lot. It made him feel good to terrify people. He thought for a moment of that girl he'd taken the raincoat from. He wished he was back there.

Bob didn't answer Vince. His heartbeats were slowing down now. The initial shock had left his muscles' feeling slack and impotent. His mind began slowly to function again.

What do I answer? he wondered. Was there an answer that would satisfy Vince, prolong the time he had to live?

He glanced over to where Stan's hands moved gently over Jane's forehead. Why had Stan done this to him?

"I asked you something," Vince said, the anger coming again. "I'm not going to wait much longer. I won't be defied."

Bob looked at him.

"What do you want me to say, Vince?" he asked.

Vince stiffened. *Wrong answer!* The words exploded in Bob's mind and made him go rigid with new fright.

"Why do you want to kill me, Vince?" he asked quickly.

Vince's eyes slitted. Was he being tricked? Well, no one would trick him.

"You know why," he said slyly.

Yes, Bob thought, *I know why.* He did know. Because of Ruth, because Vince had hated Bob with a paranoid hatred since the day he'd married the girl Vince had wanted for himself.

"Listen, Vince," he said.

"Don't try to save yourself," Vince said. "You can't."

"You have no reason to kill me," Bob said desperately. "I haven't done you any harm."

Vince stood there looking at Bob without any expression on his face. *That's right,* his mind prodded silently. *Beg for your life; I'll stand here and listen.*

"Vince, I haven't *done* anything to you," Bob said.

The room was silent. It was warmer now that the heat was up. Vince's flannel shirt was getting hot and chafing him. *I haven't done anything to you.*

Bob's words repeated themselves in his mind and the words made Vince's lips twitch. No, he hadn't done anything; only taken away Vince's life, only taken away the only girl Vince had ever wanted, the only thing he'd ever really asked for in his life.

Momentarily he thought of Ruth as he'd met her so long ago at the party after the first Town Hall engagement.

Ruth had been sitting on a couch, all alone. Vince had wandered over, sat beside her. Nobody was paying any attention to her then, only Vince. He was the one who had introduced her to everybody, the one who had made her laugh and taken away her strangeness and timidness.

And what did he get for it? He tightened. She had married Bob and deserted him.

He swallowed. No, that wasn't what had happened.

Bob had tricked her, he had hypnotized her. Maybe even drugged her. Ruth loved *him*, not Bob. She had said it that day in the music room. Oh, maybe not in so many words, but in her eyes she had said it. She couldn't get away from Bob, that's what was wrong. She was helpless and that was why...

He refocused his eyes and realized that Bob had been talking to him all the time he'd been thinking of Ruth.

"Vince, for God's sake—" Bob said.

"Shut up," Vince told him.

Now they all sat silent, watching him; Jane and Stan next to each other on the couch, Bob on the piano bench—all their eyes on him. It made Vince a little nervous, but he liked being the center of attention. It was the way it should be. He'd always loved that last minute of the concert when he knew they were all watching him from the audience and soon he would rise and bow carefully and slowly from the waist, a thin smile on his face.

"Where's Ruth?" he asked Bob suddenly.

Bob didn't answer. He just sat there looking at Vince. And he was thinking quickly. Was Vince actually planning to go to Ruth too? His throat moved. He had to stop him.

"I'm talking to you," Vince said. "Answer me when you're—"

"Vince, put that gun away," Bob said.

"Listen!" Vince snarled. "You think I'm afraid of you? You think I'm afraid to kill you? I've already killed two men and they can only get me once for—"

The words, his own, made him stiffen. He stood there staring at them, his heart pounding.

Get him? He'd never even considered it. He feared it, yes, but never for a moment did he believe they could really catch him. He was going to kill Bob and then he and Ruth would go away and have a new life.

Die? The word made him shudder. No, he wouldn't let himself think of it.

He edged over to an armchair and sank down on it. He hadn't realized how tired he was but his muscles felt slack and dead as he relaxed. He shifted a little in the chair, rested the pistol in his lap. The pistol was getting still heavier, he realized worriedly. He shouldn't wait; he knew that. He should get it over with and go. But it was different now. Killing Harry was easy because Harry had been filthy. Killing that man in the subway had been quick, almost accidental. It was different to kill someone after you talked to them, to kill deliberately. To end a sentence, then raise your gun and fire. It was hard to kill without passion. *You see,* his mind said, *that proves I'm sane, doesn't it?*

"What are you going to do?" Jane asked, "make us *wait?*"

"You'll wait. As long as I say," Vince told her.

"What if we don't *want* to wait?" she said.

His throat moved.

"You'll wait as long as I say."

She sank back against the cushion. Was it possible it was as simple as that? Just a matter of instilling a negative reaction in his fevered mind? It did seem to work.

So long as she didn't trip, so long as she didn't fall over a block in his mind, it might work.

Bob had caught it too. At first when Jane had spoken he had stiffened and thought, *Good God, she wants him to kill me.* But then he realized it was the only way. Buying time, tricking Vince into thinking they didn't want to wait so he would make them wait.

But how long could it last? Bob's throat moved convulsively and his mouth felt dry and hot. How long before Vince would suddenly tire of waiting, rise up, on impulse, and fire his gun?

Bob's muscles tightened involuntarily. Did he dare make a jump at Vince? Was it possible that Vince would be so shocked by the move he couldn't fire in time?

The thought made Bob shiver. What if he *wasn't* too surprised to fire?

It seemed impossible, this moment of melodrama.

Just a few hours before he'd been sitting with Ruth on the living room couch listening to Ravel, everything lethargic and peaceful. Now this.

That was the trouble, he realized with sudden alarm. Now that the first shock was over he couldn't really bring himself to believe that anything was going to happen to him. He was nervous, yes, but the very core of him revolted at the thought that, in minutes, he might be killed.

How could he make himself jump at Vince when he couldn't quite believe, in his own flesh, that Vince would really shoot him? And if that were so, then jumping would bring on the very thing he wanted to avoid.

Stan sat by his wife, never moving, tense and ready. If he had to, he was telling himself, he'd shield her body with his. He knew that life would be meaningless without Jane.

But his stomach was shaking and he had the horrible feeling that if the moment came he would be so petrified with fright he couldn't budge to save her.

The room became so silent that they could even hear the slow buzzing of the electric clock in the kitchen. Soon now, Vince told himself, I'm going to shoot him. There's no point in waiting.

Bob looked nervously at his watch.

"Never mind what time it is," Vince said. "It doesn't matter to you anymore."

And yet Vince could not repress the sensation that time did matter, the feeling that if he didn't shoot soon the whole thing would be impossible. As if every second were throwing up a barrier around Bob and Stan and Jane and, if he didn't fire soon, they would be encircled, inviolate.

It was as if they were all in a play and when the moment came to shoot Bob, when the cue was given, he had to shoot or the chance was over. And he felt his throat moving. What if the time had already passed?

That was stupid!

But he found himself straining forward in the chair, his heart pounding in fright. In his mind he saw the completion of the play; the men in white bursting into the apartment and grabbing him, dragging him away screaming and kicking. And Ruth was there in the last scene too, laughing as the curtain fell.

No, that *was* stupid. He threw all those thoughts away.

He stood up again restlessly. *What are you waiting for,* the voice filled his mind.

Suddenly he stopped walking and a rattling sound filled his throat.

They were all looking toward the front hall. The doorbell was ringing again.

4:15 a.m.

Bob felt his muscles tighten. For some reason the sudden idea had occurred that it was Ruth at the door. But it couldn't be her, it *couldn't*.

He looked back. Now they were all looking at Vince.

Vince's throat moved and he stood there with a restless, nervous, stance. What was the matter with the world? Why was everything so complicated? He wanted to kill the world.

"Nobody's answering it," he told them. "The first one who makes a sound..."

He trained the gun on each of them, moving his hand in an arc from Bob to Stan to Jane and back again.

"They'll see the light under the door," Jane said.

"No," Vince said.

"What if it's the police?" Jane said. "You'd better get out the back way."

"It's not the police."

A bolt of fear had exploded in Vince's chest at Jane's words. No, it couldn't be the police! His job wasn't done yet. He needed time; *time!*

His throat moved and the gun shook as it pointed at Bob. *At least I can do this*, he thought.

The doorbell ringing, someone knocking loudly on the door now. Bob started up, then sank down nervelessly as Vince extended his right arm and the dark barrel pointed at Bob's head.

"Vince, you'd better go out the back way," Jane said. "If it's—"

"Shut up!"

"But if it's the police."

"It's not!"

"It might be, Vince," Stan had added hurriedly.

"What if it is the police?" Bob suddenly joined in. Scare him, he thought, drive him away.

Vince's eyes jerked from one to the other.

Now they were all suddenly still, dead still, and Bob felt his heart hammering.

For, in the front hall they could hear the pounding on the door; but above the pounding, a voice calling.

"Bob! Bob!"

Bob jumped to his feet.

"Ruth," he muttered, his face bone-white, a hundred frightened thoughts tearing through his brain.

Vince felt his heartbeat skip and his muscles tighten. A sudden smile lit up his gaunt, sweat-greased features. *Ruth!* She'd come to him!

He started for the hall.

"No," he suddenly heard Bob gasp and, before his startled eyes, Bob broke into a run for the hall.

"Ruth!" Bob yelled. "Ruth, get away! Get *away!*"

"Stop it!" Vince screamed.

Bob didn't stop.

"Ruth, get away!" he shouted. "Ruth, ge—"

The thunder of the gun explosion drowned out his words. Bob suddenly went lurching against the wall and bounced off, landing on one knee, a surprised expression on his face.

Vince pulled the trigger again but nothing happened. Outside, in the hall, he heard Ruth scream out Bob's name. He broke into a run for the door. Bob tried to reach up and grab his leg but Vince kicked the feebly outstretched arm and Bob toppled over on his face with a rattling gasp. As Vince leaped over his body he noticed blood, slick and red across the leather of Bob's jacket.

"Vince, *don't!*" Jane screamed as she ran toward Bob. Stan stood by the couch, immobile with shock.

Vince jerked open the front door and Ruth recoiled with a breathless cry, her eyes suddenly wide with horror.

Vince grabbed at her, forgetting the gun, and the barrel cracked across her forearm, driving a numbing bolt of pain up her arm.

Vince thrust the gun into his waistband and grabbed Ruth's arm.

"Come *in* here!" he gasped.

Wordless, staring, she was dragged into the apartment and the door slammed behind her. Then, as she was spun around, she saw Bob half in the living room, half in the hallway, crumpled on the rug with Jane kneeling over him.

"*Bob!*"

The shock was so great she could hardly speak. Instinctively, she started forward, but Vince jerked her back. She turned for a moment and looked at him with a startled, confused expression. Then she turned again and her voice broke.

"Bob, Bob," she mumbled. "I'm—"

Vince pulled her against him and, as in a nightmare, she saw his white face loom before her and felt his cold lips brush across her cheek as she twisted away instinctively.

"Ruth, *Ruth*..." Vince's voice was husky and shaking. It was Ruth, his Ruth; she had come to him. Ruth felt his lean body press into hers and she thought she was going to scream. Over Vince's shoulder she saw Bob lying there on the rug and Jane looking up now, her face white.

Jane saw that Vince's back was turned. Abruptly she pushed up from the floor. Stan jerked out his hand and caught her wrist.

"What are you doing?" he whispered in fright.

"Let go!" she hissed back.

She tore from his grasp and started for the bedroom.

Stan jumped up, his face slack, and ran around the couch edge. He reached the door a second before she did.

"Don't be insane!" he begged her in a hoarse whisper. "You saw what he did to Bob!"

"God *damn* you!" Her voice was a crackling mutter of hate.

Her eyes fled to the hall. Then, suddenly, she turned and ran dizzily across the living room, her head aching. Stan started toward her but she reached the phone first and jerked up the receiver.

Dead. She'd forgotten the living room phone was only an extension from the bedroom connection; the one Vince had ripped out.

Suddenly all the fury and hate exploded in a scream that tore from her lips.

"I'll *kill* him!"

With a wrenching sob she shoved aside Stan and started running for the kitchen.

In the hall, Vince heard her scream and, suddenly, he shoved Ruth aside. She crashed into the wall with a gasp and Vince grabbed his gun. He raced past Ruth into the living room, jumping over Bob's motionless body.

Ruth pushed away from the wall and moved on trembling legs toward her husband.

Jane was pulling out a kitchen drawer as Vince came in. Without a thought he jumped toward her and pushed her against a cabinet. She whirled with a sob, a carving knife clutched in her right hand.

"I'll *kill* you!" she screamed in his face.

The gun clattered to the floor unheeded as he grabbed for her wrist.

"*Vince!*" he heard Stan cry from the kitchen doorway.

Vince's mind erupted. The world was trying to trap him! For a moment he and Jane strained against each other. Then, with a vicious snarl, he drove his knee up into Jane's stomach and she doubled over with a retching gag. The knife went skidding across the cabinet top and clattered into the sink.

Then, as Vince whirled, he saw Stan on his knees grabbing at the gun.

With a grunt he brought up his knee again, this time into Stan's face. Stan went flailing back onto the linoleum, striking his head against the bottom of a cabinet door.

Vince grabbed up the gun, pointed it at Stan's chest, and pulled the trigger. There was only a clicking sound as the hammer hit. Vince pulled the trigger again, again.

Empty.

With a howl of berserk fury he flung the gun with all his might at Stan; but his aim was bad and the gun bounced off the cabinet door and skidded across the linoleum.

Vince scuttled back until he banged against the sink cabinet. His left arm was pinned against the edge and he gasped at the pain. Gritting his teeth, his shaking fingers moved into the sink and drew out the long knife.

He stood there shaking, looking down at the two of them writhing on the floor. His thin chest shuddered with breaths and he could feel warm drops of blood running down his arm again.

Jane half sat, half lay against the sink cabinet, her legs drawn up, her hands pressed into her stomach. Her face was white, her open mouth gasping for breath. Little sounds of gagging agony sounded in her throat as she writhed in pain. A cough burst through her lips, racking and dry.

Stan struggled to his knees, moaning from the pain. It had been like a spike driven into his brain. For a moment he had blacked out and thought he was going to die. Then the sounds and sights of the kitchen had flickered back to him again—Vince leaning against the sink, panting, the long knife sticking out from his right hand, Jane lying there and...

Stan started up.

"Jane," he mumbled in a thick voice.

"Get up," Vince gasped. "Get up."

As Stan stood on wobbling legs, Vince backed into the living room. He lowered the knife until he held it at his side, pointing at Stan.

Then Vince glanced over to where Ruth was kneeling by Bob, sobbing and trying to stop the bleeding with her fingers.

"Get to you in a—in a minute," Vince gasped.

He turned to Stan. Stan was trying to help Jane to her feet but she couldn't get up. Vince's head whipped around. What was he going to do? There were too many people to keep track of; he had to make them go away. He wanted to be alone with Ruth.

The bathroom.

"You..." he said, forgetting Stan's name for a moment, "you...*Stan*. Take her in the bathroom."

Stan looked at him with sick, frightened eyes.

"What?" he asked, a break in his voice.

"Get her in the *bathroom*, I said!" Vince said loudly. Why didn't anyone *listen* to him?

Stan leaned over Jane.

"Honey," he said brokenly. "Honey. We—"

Vince watched him, trembling with anger when nothing happened.

"God damn it, get her up!"

He started toward the kitchen, then looked at Ruth again. She was looking at him, her face white and drawn.

"Vince," she murmured, "help..."

He raised his right hand to let her know he'd be with her in a second. He saw the knife blade pointing at her and drew it down quickly.

"I'll, I'll, I'll—" he stuttered nervously and almost felt as if he were going to cry. Everything was so complex and nerve-wracking.

"*Vince!*" Ruth begged.

He didn't hear her. He was looking at Stan.

"Damn it!" he cried furiously, "*get her up!*"

Stan tried to, but Jane's legs were curled up to keep the pressure off her stomach.

"Get away," she groaned. "Get away."

Tears of pain ran down her cheeks.

"Honey, we've got to..."

He gasped and jolted to the side as he felt something cold and thin jab into his shoulder. He stood against the sink trembling, feeling blood trickle down his back and the wild sensation of pain in his right shoulder.

Vince bent over Jane and stuck the point of the knife to her throat.

"Get up, get up!" he ordered, his voice shrill in the tiny kitchen.

"Vince, don't..." Stan sobbed.

Jane looked up at Vince, her mouth still open, gasping for breath.

Suddenly Vince grabbed her hair with his left hand. A bolt of pain raged up the arm and he let go with a gasp. Still holding the knife, he grabbed Jane's dark hair with his other hand and tried to drag her to her feet. She'd get out of here if he had to drag her out himself!

A breathless cry of pain twisted Jane's lips as Vince pulled her up.

"Get up, I said!"

Vince backed away as she stumbled into the sink with a sob of pain and Stan caught her around the waist with one trembling arm. The two of them stood there shaking without control, driven and afraid. All subtleties had gone from their minds; they were two hurt, frightened animals; the eyes they watched him with were dumb and uncalculating with fright.

"Get in the bathroom," Vince said.

He backed into the living room but they still stood there as if they didn't understand him.

Hot tears flew from Vince's eyes as he leaped forward with a gagging curse.

"God damn it!" he screamed at them. "Are you—"

"Don't hurt us!" Stan begged.

Vince backed away, shivering, while they came stumbling out of the kitchen. Jane bent over clutching her stomach. Stan, eyes wide and dumb, stared at Vince.

Ruth gasped as they came out. She couldn't understand it; it was like a senseless, incredible dream. From the moment she'd seen Vince, then Bob lying on the floor, her mind wouldn't function. Thoughts jumbled one on top of the other.

"Stan," she muttered, "Jane…"

She knelt there, looking first at them, then at Bob's white face, at the blood running across the leather jacket and around his still body to the floor.

"Go on, go on," Vince snapped in a jaded voice.

Vince's mind felt numbed now. Too many things had happened. He didn't want to think; it was too painful. There was only one thing he wanted to worry about. Ruth and him going away and…

"I'll be right out," he told Ruth in what he thought was a comforting tone.

She stared at him unbelievingly.

Then, with a gasp, she stood and ran for the hall. *I have to get help!* The words burst in her brain, the first coherent thought she'd had since Vince had opened the door.

She turned in numbed surprise as Vince grabbed her coat and pulled her back.

"You're not going away?" he asked, surprise in his voice, incredulous surprise.

For a second she stared at him blankly.

"I—I have to get help," she said feebly. She didn't understand.

"No," he said as if he were reasoning with her. "No, Ruth. You and I…"

She still didn't understand. She tried to pull away but he held on to her. She stared at him, face still expressionless, eyes wide and uncomprehending.

"Ruth, you and I…" he started again.

"But I have to get help!" she suddenly burst out. "My husband is hurt!"

She recoiled as his face twisted angrily.

"You're not going anywhere!" he snapped. "I killed him for you and—"

"*You!*"

She backed into the wall with a shudder.

Vince's throat moved. He wouldn't let himself believe that look of horror on her face. He grabbed at her wrist.

"Get in there," he said.

She froze against the wall, staring at him.

"I said get *in* there!"

His voice broke and he almost started crying. Why wouldn't she do what he asked? What was the matter with her? It was obvious that he'd only killed Bob to help her.

Her body shuddered as Vince half dragged her into the living room. Stan and Jane were still there, Stan leaning against the bedroom door and supporting Jane, who still bent over, hands clutched over her stomach.

"I said get in the bathroom," Vince ordered.

He pulled Ruth back from Bob.

"He's hurt!" she cried out at him.

"He's dead! Leave him alone!" Vince cried back at her.

Her white hands pressed into her cheeks.

"*No.*"

Stan moved across the bedroom staggering because he had to almost carry Jane.

Vince pulled Ruth into the bedroom.

"No," she muttered in a dead voice. "No, he isn't."

"He *is,* he *is,*" Vince insisted, then looked at Stan.

"Get in there!"

He pushed Ruth toward a bed.

"Sit there," he said.

She tried to rush for the living room but he stood in her path and drove his left hand across her cheek. They both gasped at the same time, she from surprise, he from pain.

She backed away with a whimper.

"Sit down, Ruth," he said.

Her brain wouldn't work. She stood there staring at him, her heart pounding in great, body-shaking beats.

"Sit *down.*"

Vince wanted to cry because nobody would do what he asked. He wanted to be nice to her and make her happy. What was wrong with her?

Now he heard the sound of the toilet cover in the bathroom being knocked down.

Vince moved across the bedroom and flicked on the bathroom light. He saw Jane sitting down and Stan turned, blinking, his face very white.

"Close the door," Vince told him. "Lock it."

"Huh?"

Vince pulled the door shut. As he waited he looked toward Ruth.

"Don't move," he told her. "I don't want to hurt you."

He turned back.

"*Lock* it!" he yelled.

He heard the door being locked. Then he looked around and found a chair. He propped the back of it underneath the knob and kicked it in tight.

There. They were out of the way.

He turned for Ruth.

4:35 a.m.

The two maiden ladies came marching up the steps, obdurate, thin-lipped with puritanical ire. They wore their robes up to the top of their necks, their respectability to the tops of their heads.

"I think we've had just about enough from the Sheldons," said one, her voice acid with a righteous disgust.

"It's time their *parties* were reported to the authorities," said the other.

"Parties indeed!" the other woman joined in. "More like..."

She looked over her shoulder lest someone be found trailing them. Then she looked back at her sister.

"*Orgies.*"

Her lips framed the word; she dared not speak it aloud.

"Wouldn't be surprised," said the other. "Not a bit. That *lady* he married. She's just a..."

Her eyes too moved over one shoulder.

"Hussy," she finished, satisfied that no one lurked behind, taking notes.

The two of them reached the top of the flight and moved across the hall toward the door.

"Almost five in the morning," said one of them, "and still they're at it; banging on the piano and knocking over furniture and breaking bottles and screaming at the top of their lungs. It's a disgrace, I tell you, a disgrace."

"They're probably just having a little *fun*," snapped the other.

"*Uh*," was all her sister replied.

They stood before the door and one of them pushed in the doorbell button.

They stood there waiting for someone to answer.

"He'll probably be drunk when he comes to the door," one predicted ruthlessly.

"I hope it's not *her*," said the other. "I don't even want to *look* at her."

"Hussy," murmured the first.

No one came to the door. Inside, they thought they heard a cry, then only silence.

"I'm sure you're having a good time," said the one addressing the revelers she imagined within, "but we're not leaving here until you open the door."

They both nodded once, sternly in agreement.

Silence inside. The two maiden ladies shuffled blue and pink mules on the cold hall floor. Each held the same posture; each held the top of her robe shut at the throat with a clenched right hand. Each seethed with indignation.

"Well, of all the...!" one finally snapped angrily.

"I *never*..." said the other.

"Probably too *busy* to answer."

The first held her finger against the bell.

"Well, you'll answer," she said sharply to the sybarites she envisioned in every corner of the apartment. "You'll answer if we have to—to *ring* your brains out!"

They both nodded once. They liked the phrase. Ring them out. Toll out the evil and the blackness, burn out the...

"Who's there?" they heard a voice inside.

The turkey throat of the first woman moved.

"Kindly open the door, Mr. Sheldon," said the woman.

"Who is it?"

The first looked at the second. Her lips framed the words, *"That's not Mr. Sheldon."*

"We're from apartment 7-c," said the second woman. "We live in the apartment below and you're keeping us awake with your *party.*"

The way she said *party* made them both nod vigorously. Whoever it was inside could not fail to recognize, they knew, the acidity in the pronunciation of the word.

"There's no party," they heard the voice inside say.

"We would like to speak to Mr. Sheldon," said the first maiden lady. "We feel—"

"He's *sick,*" interrupted the voice. "He can't see anyone."

Sick. The first framed the word with her lips and the second nodded with a bitter smile. They knew what *sick* meant.

"I'm sorry but we must demand silence," said the second woman, taking the reins in her hand. "We cannot—"

"Go away!"

"Oh!"

They stood there trembling with outrage.

"Very well," said the first. "Perhaps we'll just call the police then and—"

"Don't!" cried the voice inside.

The old ladies smiled and nodded to themselves. There, that had put the fear of God in him.

But the door stayed shut.

"Maybe he thinks he's having a great laugh on us," one muttered to the second, visualizing the man inside doubled over with scornful laughter.

The other one spoke, supposedly to her sister, but, actually, directly at the door.

"Well, come along, Nell," she said. "I guess we'll just have to call the police then."

They stood there a moment longer. Then with a firming of lips, a stiffening of backs, they moved slowly away from the door.

"'Well, did you ever?" muttered the first as they reached the steps.

"No. I never," responded the other. "Should we call the police do you think?"

"I—think we should."

But they weren't sure. They didn't want to get involved in any trouble. They lived a simple, cloistered life and they didn't want police asking them questions. Especially on the Sabbath.

As they started down the steps one of them stopped.

"Good heavens," she said, leaning over to squint at the steps, "what are those spots?"

The other one looked, gasped.

"They look like..."

*　　*　　*

Vince lay against the door until the sound of their footsteps had shuffled away. Then his throat moved and he pushed away from the door. They were going to call the police! He had to get Ruth and get away.

I hope I didn't hurt her, he thought anxiously as he moved down the hallway.

When the doorbell had rung Ruth had cried out, tried to run to the door and answer it. Vince had struck her to make her quiet.

Why did he keep hurting people? All he wanted to do was live with Ruth and be happy. And all he did was hurt people. Some people didn't matter, of course. Harry didn't matter and Bob didn't matter. But he didn't mean to hurt the man in the subway station or to hurt Stan or...Well, Jane, he didn't care about.

Then, as he started into the living room he gasped and stopped in his tracks.

Bob was looking at him.

Vince stood there rigidly looking down at him. *He's dead,* his mind said. *He's dead and he's staring at me.*

"V—V—Vince."

Bob groped for speech, the word thick and sticky in his throat.

"No." Vince cowered away.

"Vince."

Vince edged around Bob into the living room. He couldn't touch Bob now. It was different. Before it hadn't been so bad. Bob had tried to send Ruth away and he shouldn't have done that; Vince was forced to shoot him.

But now it was different. He didn't want to touch Bob; he didn't even want to look at him.

"Vince...h—help."

"No," Vince muttered, "no."

"Vince."

"No, leave me alone," Vince gasped. "No, I don't want to..."

He ran into the bedroom and shut the door again. He leaned against it, shaking. Why didn't anything go right? Why wasn't Bob dead like he should be?

"I—didn't mean to..." he muttered, but he didn't know what he meant by that.

Carefully he locked the door and moved over to where Ruth lay sprawled across the bed on her back. He had to hurry; they had to go before the police came.

Quickly he felt for her pulse. His throat moved. She was all right. He straightened up. He should get a wet rag and wipe her face. But he couldn't use the bathroom because

Stan and Jane were there. And, if he went to the kitchen he'd have to go past Bob again. He didn't want to do that either. Vince was afraid. Suddenly, all rage and violent hate had gone from him. He was afraid and nervous.

He sat down beside Ruth and held her hand. He looked at her still face. His eyes grew pained when he saw the bruise where he'd struck her on the jaw. He shouldn't have hit her. But if he hadn't she would have run into the hall. Why? What was the matter with her?

He stroked her hand slowly and his throat moved.

"Ruth?" he said. Timidly.

He started to bend over to kiss her but then he straightened up. No, he'd wait. Until she'd wake up and smile at him and kiss him and they'd go away together and start a new life.

"Just you and me, Ruth," he said to her as if she could hear. "We'll go somewhere—together. Some little place, somewhere. Some town, you know, maybe in Ohio. It doesn't matter, maybe Missouri. I can get a job in a bar maybe or a roadhouse. I can play the piano and we'll have our secret and we'll get a little house to live in. And maybe I'll give a concert and—well, anyway we'll have a little house. And—and we'll be happy."

He sat there looking at her as if he wanted her to answer him. He forgot about the police coming. He was content to sit there with her.

Abstractedly his eyes moved down from her face, over her chest.

He drew them back conscious of looking. No, that wasn't right, he wasn't that way. They were going to get married and be happy together. Vince's throat moved and he drew in shaking breaths. He tried to ignore the hot feeling in his stomach, the feeling he knew so well. He shuddered.

He looked down. *She looks hot,* his mind said. *It's hot in here. I better open her coat or she'll get overheated and then she'll catch a cold when we go to the train and...*

Nervously, hands shaking, he undid the belt of her coat and lay the coat open on both sides.

"There," he muttered.

Then, guiltily, his eyes moved toward the bathroom. Could they see him through the keyhole? He swallowed and felt a sinking sensation in his stomach.

No, the chair covered the keyhole; and the bedroom door was locked. He was safe with her, alone with her. No one could get in and...

"No."

He muttered it again, defying himself, becoming frightened at the heat that was crawling along his limbs. His arm ached and he felt a hot flush moving up his cheeks. *No, no.* His hands twitched on his lap. He reached out to touch her, stopped. A tight, hot ball was forming in his stomach. No, it wasn't right.

His eyes moved down over her body. A harsh breath burst from his nostrils. She had on only a thin sweater over her brassiere. He could see the movement of her breasts as she breathed. He watched them rise and fall.

"No," he muttered.

But he couldn't stop. He stared at her body. After all, his mind reasoned weakly, we're going to get married. I'm going to be her husband and we...

His throat moved harshly. His hand reached out, he jerked it back again.

"No, I just..." he started, then broke off into a pitiful moan.

What was the matter with her? His mind went off on a new tack. She should know better than to wear such a tight sweater on her body. That wasn't nice. Any girl who did that was...

Trying bores, Vincent, disgusting filth!

He twisted in actual pain on the bed. His arm throbbed and felt as if it were expanding.

He turned away with a hiss. He closed his eyes and shook without control as he sat there.

Abruptly then, he turned back and slapped her face. He grabbed her by the hair and shook her.

"Wake *up,*" he said, almost angrily, almost resenting her being such a temptation. "Wake up. Don't you see we..."

His hand moved out and touched her breast.

He pulled it away with a whimper, a tingling sensation in his fingers. No! Wrong, dirty, *dirty!*

He clenched his fists until his left arm ached and burned. I'll punish myself! I'll cut off my hand and—

Something snapped. He turned and looked over her body, his chest rising and falling in shaking movements.

And, suddenly, with a wretched sob, he dug his fingers beneath the neck of her sweater, jerked with all his might, and ripped it off her body.

"Ruth...!"

His voice was a gasp, a snarl, a shuddering ache of sound.

4:40 a.m.

He held a cold, wet washcloth against Jane's forehead. She sat erect, her face still white, her hands still over her stomach.

"How...are you?" he asked.

She didn't answer. She took a ragged breath and didn't even look at him.

His eyes fell.

"You may as well be nice to me," he muttered. "We'll probably both be dead soon."

He'd meant that to sound cynically brave, but the words made him shudder. He stood up.

"Floor's cold," he said.

She sat there staring at the wall.

"What should we do?" he said, just to say something. He knew very well there was nothing they could do.

"Why don't you jump out the window?" she said bitterly.

His lips pressed together. He turned away from her and looked at the window.

Jane looked up in surprise as Stan clambered into the bathtub and pushed up the window.

As he looked out Stan could see that there was a six-inch ledge that led along the building to the window that opened on the eighth floor hallway.

His stomach fell as he looked down at the street, murky grey in the early morning. What would she say if I *did* jump, he wondered.

"I could," he said, thinking aloud.

"Shut that window," she said irritably. "There's a draft."

His throat moved and he turned to face her.

"I could get out," he said. "If..."

She looked at him blankly.

"What are you talking about?"

He licked his lips.

"The window," he said. "There's a ledge."

With a grunt of pain she stood and moved for the bathtub, grimacing as she walked. He stepped aside and she lifted one leg over the edge of the tub with an indrawn breath. Stan took her arm and supported her and she didn't pull away or say anything.

She looked out.

"My God there *is,*" she said, suddenly excited.

She looked at him quickly and he felt his muscles tighten. There was no scorn in her face, no reviling.

"Do you think you could?" she asked.

He swallowed and stared at her. He was sorry he'd mentioned it. He'd never thought...

She turned away, her face falling into its old, bitter lines. He reached out impulsively and caught her arm.

"I could," he said, "if—if you asked me."

For a moment they looked directly at each other and something flickered between them, something that had not been a part of their relationship for years.

"Stan," she said.

He tensed himself.

"I'll go," he said.

She looked at him for another moment.

"Hurry then," she said.

Stan stepped out of his slippers and stood on the cold porcelain of the tub. Then he took a deep breath and, holding onto the window ledge, he stepped up on the side of the tub. He almost slipped, then his toes caught hold. He stood there, his heart hammering, looking down at the grey pit that was Manhattan before dawn. He swallowed hard.

Before the feeling got worse, he put one leg over the windowsill.

As he did they heard the doorbell ring.

Stan stopped moving and they looked at each other.

"Who's that?" Stan muttered.

She shook her head once and they listened. As Stan drew back his leg they heard a sound of feet running in the bedroom, then a muffled cry. Silence for a moment, more footsteps, and the bedroom door shut.

In silence, they stood there listening.

The next thing they heard was the bedroom door opening and closing again. Then, in a moment, the sound of a muffled voice in the bedroom, Vince talking to Ruth.

A sudden coldness covered Stan. For a moment he'd hoped it was the police and that he wouldn't have to climb out the window.

"It was probably those two biddies downstairs," Jane said, "coming to complain about the noise."

"Oh, God," Stan said bitterly. "And I bet they were too stupid to realize something was wrong."

Jane's smile was as bitter as his voice.

"Noise from our place is nothing new to them," she said.

They were silent a moment. Then she said, "You'd better go. And *hurry*. When I felt Bob's heart before he was still alive. There may still be a chance to save him. I don't think Vince will do anything to Ruth."

Stan looked at her a moment. Then he nodded and lowered his head so she wouldn't see that he was afraid.

He put his leg over the sill again, then drew up the other until he was sitting on the windowsill, his legs hanging out the window. He felt a cold morning wind blowing over his legs.

He gripped the window ledge more tightly. "Well..." he said.

But there wasn't any more to say. He turned over onto his stomach with a straining of muscles. A dull pain started in his shoulder where Vince had jabbed him with the knife. He'd forgotten about it.

The cold wind rushed over him as he lowered his feet slowly down toward the ledge, his face red and taut from the strain.

"Where's the ledge?" he muttered nervously.

His bare feet touched the cold concrete ledge and he swallowed. He raised his eyes and looked in at her.

A smile flickered over her lips. It had been so long since she'd smiled at him and meant it. It was hard.

"Be careful," she said and it made him want to cry out in joy.

"I will," he said and moved away from the window. He held on to the window edge as long as he could. Then he stopped. *Don't look down*, he told himself. He felt his heart beating rapidly. The wind gushed around his body and tried to push him off the ledge.

He saw he would have to let go of the bathroom window and lunge for a grip on the hall window.

But what if it were locked? The thought made his heart stop for a second.

He stood there taking deep breaths of the cold air. It flooded down his throat, chilling him. He wanted to cry out. But he knew he couldn't; not now. He couldn't crawl back into the bathroom, abject and defeated, and face Jane. He just couldn't bear to lose the faith she seemed to have in him now.

He stood there on the ledge shaking and holding onto the bathroom window edge with rigid fingers.

"Are you all right?" he heard Jane ask.

His throat moved and he bit his lip.

"Yes," he answered weakly, "all right."

He looked toward the hall window. There was nothing to grab. He stood staring at the window. There had to be something!

Tentatively he stretched out his right leg. He could just touch the other window with his toes.

There was no getting away from it. He'd have to move along the ledge hugging the wall until he stood before the hall window.

He caught his breath, held it. And let go of the bathroom window.

For one horrible moment he thought he was going to fall. But it was only an illusion fostered by fear. He leaned into the building and clutched at the rough stone with his nails.

Now he moved his right foot cautiously along the edge. The cold wind still blew over him. He moved his left foot, then his right again, sliding it over the cold, rough concrete. His stomach moved and he thought maybe he was going to be sick. He swallowed the feeling, repressing it. *God help me.*

He reached the window. He stood before it and, slowly, his right hand edged up to the inside edge of the window under the lock. His fingers tensed, he tried to push up the window.

It was locked.

* * *

With a groan Bob raised himself on one elbow, a clicking sound in his throat. Blood still trickled over his jacket and he felt as if his shoulder and back were on fire. The room swam around him and he blinked. Sweat ran down into his eyes and he tried to shake his head but the movement made his shoulder and back hurt too much.

His throat moved convulsively and he gasped for breath. He had to get help.

Ruth. Where was she? She must be in the bedroom with Vince. He had to get help. Now, now...

He started to drag himself toward the front door. As he did a rushing wave of blackness dashed over him and almost drew him under. He gritted his teeth and tensed himself. *I mustn't black out. I mustn't!*

He started crawling for the door, trailing blood behind him on the rug.

He was halfway to the door when he heard Ruth's scream from the bedroom.

*　　*　　*

Jane whirled from the window when she heard the scream. As she moved toward the door she heard Vince's angry voice and then a sound of struggling in the bedroom.

He's killing her! The thought burst in her mind and she felt her heart catch.

Suddenly she found herself at the door. She turned the lock quickly and shoved. The door was blocked. She rammed her weight against the door and felt the flaring of pain in her stomach and head.

Then the chair fell over and Jane half fell into the bedroom.

Vince started up from the bed looking frightened and guilty. Ruth was pushed back against the head of the bed, one arm across her exposed breasts, the other raised up to ward off a blow.

Sex. The word jerked across Jane's mind as she saw them. And it suddenly seemed as if the answer were obvious. With a rasping sob, Vince grabbed up the knife and turned back to Jane.

Jane calmly, slowly, as if it were something she had planned for all her life, let down the straps of her nightgown.

"Vincie," she said in a low voice.

Vince felt his stomach muscles jerk in at the sound of her voice. He stared helplessly as the soft folds of the robe dropped to the floor and Jane was naked to the waist. His throat moved convulsively and he found himself backing away a step.

"Come to me, Vincie," Jane murmured, writhing her body a little bit. "Come to me."

The hot flush on Vince's cheeks flamed into life again. He felt breath shaking in his chest. *No, no,* the voice he heard in his brain was weak and without conviction. He stared at her with sick, hungry eyes.

Then Jane moved her right hip a little and the gown rustled to the rug. She stepped out of the crumpled black folds, arms stretched out. This is my fate, she thought as she moved for Vince.

"You don't want her," she heard herself saying. "She's not the kind you like. She's no fun, Vincie. I'm fun. I'm a *lot* of fun."

"No..." muttered Vince. He felt himself raising the knife as if he were going to attack Jane.

Ruth looked at Jane with stark, frightened eyes that didn't understand. It was hard for her to breathe.

Now Jane was between the two beds. She took a deep breath and the hard points of her breasts rose. "Come here, baby," she muttered. She couldn't look at Ruth. She had the terrible feeling that she'd start to cry helplessly if she looked at Ruth.

"I'm waiting, baby," she said and edged closer to the table.

Vince moved toward her. *I don't care,* he heard a voice in him. *I'm going to...*

There was no heat in Jane's body. The tautness of her flesh was the rigidity of frozen things, of cold calculation. Her body meant nothing; it was only a tool, a means to an end. As long as she didn't look at Ruth.

Vince was too close, she suddenly realized. Too close; there was not enough time.

"Come to me, come to me," she murmured quickly. "Never mind her. Let her *watch.*"

Ruth stared with stricken eyes at Jane, at her tight, ruthless face. She couldn't. *Oh, Jane, Jane...*

Jane's smooth arm slid around Vince's back. His lean body came close and she pushed against him. Her mouth opened as it closed over his. She felt the handle of the knife bruising her back as Vince embraced her.

One of her hands left Vince's back and, rapidly, gestured toward the door. Ruth caught her breath, suddenly understanding, hating herself for a second for not understanding. As quietly as she could, her heart pounding, she edged across the bed. Jane's hand moved down to the drawer now. She eased it open while, with her other arm, she held Vince's body close, kept his face against hers with her clinging, biting lips. She hardly felt his left hand moving up her chest. She felt almost numb.

Then she jerked at the pistol.

A spear of ice impaled her as the barrel got caught on the drawer. Vince suddenly pulled away and looked down. His heart seemed to jolt in his chest. His pupils expanded suddenly and he knew that he'd been tricked again, lied to.

"No!" he screamed at her. Jane recoiled in sudden fear as he lunged with the knife. At the door, Ruth screamed.

*   *   *

Stan pounded on the front door, his wrist still running blood from the gash he'd gotten punching in the hall window.

He turned away with a gasp. What am I going to do? He turned back with a sudden whine and threw himself bodily against the door. No use! He felt a surge of terror and uselessness at not being able to get in and protect her.

He rushed down the hall to the door of the apartment across the way. He rang the bell and pounded on the door.

"Help!" he yelled. "Help!"

Then the door of his own apartment opened and Bob came staggering out. With a startled gasp, Stan jumped forward and raced down to where Bob had sunk to one knee, blood spattering on the hall floor.

"Bob, are you...?"

Without finishing the question he looked into the apartment. Where was she?

He started to bend over to help Bob up, but Ruth's scream and a crashing sound in the bedroom jolted him up. He dove into the apartment.

As he reached the bedroom door he heard it being locked.

"Jane!" he cried brokenly. *"Jane!"*

"Get away!" he heard Vince yell. "I'll kill you if you don't get away!"

A whining breath broke from Stan's lips and, with a berserk cry, he lunged at the door, driving his broad shoulder into it. It didn't move. He pounded his fists on the door.

"Jane!"

He backed up and ran at the door. It shuddered under the impact. He moved back again and crashed his large body into it. The lock snapped and he went rushing into the bedroom. As he did he saw the white face of Vince flash by, the figure of Ruth standing by the bed.

Then, as he stopped himself and spun around he saw Vince run out the opened doorway and into the hall.

And, suddenly, with a gagging cry, he saw Jane lying crumpled on the floor, the lamp shattered around her.

The knife handle sticking out from her chest.

He stood there petrified for a long moment, his eyes wide and unbelieving. Then, abruptly, a cracking sob shook him and he ran to her.

"Jane..."

Ruth looked at him as he stumbled over and knelt by Jane. Then she ran from the room.

Stan put his hand on the knife handle, then his fingers twitched away. He felt a great pressure on his brain as if someone were holding huge, hot hands against his skull and pressing. The room seemed to twist and contort out of shape. He almost fainted.

"Jane," he mumbled. *"Jane."*

Like a child trying to wake its mother.

Her eyes opened; slowly, with a painful fluttering.

"Jane, you're—all right." The last word spoken feebly in the realization that all hope was gone.

Her throat moved and she made a clicking sound.

"Jane, I'll get a doctor," he suddenly gasped.

Her hand closed weakly on his pajama leg, holding him. Her lips moved as if she were trying to speak. But no sound came at first.

Then she said, "No."

"Jane, I…"

She made a tiny hushing sound as if she would silence all his fear and terror.

"You—" a gasping intake of breath, "—be better now."

"Jane!"

"Please." Her throat moved and she grimaced at the pain.

"I'll call a doctor!"

"No, no." She pressed her lips together. The lipstick was all smeared and caked.

"You…"

Again her throat moved. She could hardly breathe.

"Stan?"

He bent over, tears rolling down his cheeks.

"W-what, darling? What?"

"Kiss me."

His sob shook his body.

"Please," she whispered, then her face suddenly grew taut. *"Now,"* she said.

He bent over and placed his shaking mouth on hers. Her fingers tightened on his pajama leg. Her lips parted.

She died as he kissed her.

*   *   *

When Vince came rushing out of the apartment he saw Bob still on one knee in the hall. With a gasp he lunged past Bob and started racing down the hall, his black shoes clicking on the tiles.

As he passed another door, it opened and a man in a bathrobe came out.

"Now what—" he started to say, then his head snapped as Vince rushed past him.

Vince reached the stairs and started racing down. He kept sobbing and whimpering in fright as he descended. Half way down the flight he almost tripped and his right arm shot out to grab the banister. His shoes slipped on the edge of a step and he skidded down on his side, holding on to the banister with clawing fingers.

Caught!

The word knifed at his brain as he ran down the steps. No escape! Everybody was against him! Bob was alive and Ruth wasn't going away with him. Nothing was right! Hot tears of futility scalded down his cheeks as he ran and the stairs looked like gelatin through the quivering lenses of his tears. Lost, lost, lost!

"Saul," he gasped, "help me, Saul."

Then, at the fourth floor, he suddenly skidded to a halt, his breath caught.

With unbelieving eyes he looked down the stair well and saw the police officers running up toward him.

For a moment he couldn't move. He stood there dizzily, staring at them.

Then a sob broke in his throat and, whirling, he started up the steps again.

Fifth floor, around to the stairs; sixth floor, around to the stairs; seventh floor. His breath burst from open mouth now, there was a stitch jabbing a hot spear into his side; his breaths were choking wheezes.

The eighth floor. He stopped for breath and looked toward the apartment.

Bob was gone, the man was gone. He saw the door of the other apartment open and heard Ruth's voice inside. Then he looked suddenly at Stan's apartment.

Stan was in the doorway looking at him.

"Stan?" he said.

Stan stood there and Vince started toward him suddenly.

"Stan, don't let them…"

He recoiled with a gasp as Stan came at him with the bloodstained knife in his hand.

With a sob, he whirled and started up the last flight of steps to the roof. He heard Stan break into a run, his bare feet thudding on the hall floor.

Vince fumbled at the hook on the heavy door with a sound of fury.

"Open," he told the door in a frenzied whisper. *"Open!"*

Just before Stan reached him he knocked the thick hook off and shoved open the door. Stan's lunge didn't reach and Stan toppled forward on the gravel-topped roof.

Stan got to his knees, ignoring his torn pajamas, his bruised knees, the gashes he'd gotten on his wrist punching in the window. Everything in the world had disappeared but Vince; every hope, sensation, every fear. There was nothing but Vince racing across the roof, his shoes scrabbling on the gravel, his white face looking back over his shoulder as he ran.

Stan started forward. Slowly. There was no place Vince could go; no roof adjoined the apartment house. His bare feet moved and crunched over the gravel, his face stolid. His fingers tightened on the knife.

Vince reached the edge of the roof and whirled. Stan was coming toward him over the roof, the knife held at his side. Vince could see blood running down Stan's arm and dripping off the tip of the sharp blade. He could see Stan's face, white and like the mask of a dead man.

"Stan, no!" he yelled. "Stan, I didn't hurt you! Stan, don't do any—"

He leaped to the side and Stan went crashing into the side of the roof, almost toppling over the edge.

Stan turned, his face blank. He started toward Vince again.

"Stan," Vince muttered.

He ran a little ways across the roof, then turned.

"Stan, don't hurt me," he begged, tears rushing down his cheeks. "Stan, *please* don't hurt me!"

Stan raised the knife slowly.

Vince turned and ran again toward the door.

Then he recoiled and his shoes skidded on the gravel as two police officers came lunging through the doorway, pistols in their hands.

"*No!*" he cried.

Now he was caught between them. He ran to the side and stood with his back to the waist-high wall.

One of the officers moved toward him. The other moved toward Stan.

"Give me the knife, buddy," he said, stretching out his free hand.

"*No,*" gagged Stan and he lunged toward Vince. Vince shrank back against the wall.

"No," he muttered in a terrified voice. "No, it isn't fair. It isn't fair."

He pushed himself up on the wall until he was sitting on the edge. Stan tore away from the policeman's hold and jumped at Vince.

"*Don't!*" Vince screamed at him, screamed at the world.

Then he was gone.

And, when they reached the edge of the roof, they saw his body falling, his arms and legs kicking and flailing as he plummeted toward the sidewalk, his screams of horror echoing between the silent buildings.

5:00 a.m.

Ruth turned away from the stairs as the two men carried Bob down to the ambulance on a stretcher.

"Nothing fatal," the interne had assured her. "He'll be all right."

And Bob had smiled weakly at her, gripped her hand and she had told him she'd be right down to the hospital with him.

Now she walked back to the apartment.

Stan was in the bedroom. He'd put Jane on the bed and covered her up, all but her face. He was sitting beside her and staring at her.

He glanced at Ruth as she came in, his face dead and slack.

She put her hand on his shoulder.

"Stan," she said.

His throat moved.

"She was brave," was all he said.

"I—" She looked at him. "Yes," she said then, "she was."

Stan's head lowered and she stood there looking at him, feeling helpless before his sorrow.

"If there's anything..." she started.

"Thank you," he said hollowly.

She turned away and heard his tightly restrained sob.

And when she reached the street, she saw the two orderlies putting another stretcher into the ambulance, a stretcher that was completely covered.

The two officers got back in their patrol car.

"Yeah," said one, "I remember the case. The kid cracked up and killed his old man with a letter opener. Then he went to the office of this guy that was shot and he tried to kill him too. They put him away."

He made a grim sound.

"I guess he got away," he said.

"Well, he won't be killing anybody else," said the other one.

"No," said the first, "he won't."

And he shook his head.

"What a world," he said.

Forty minutes later the sun came up.

THE END

If you've enjoyed this book, you will not want to miss these terrific titles...

ARMCHAIR SCI-FI & HORROR DOUBLE NOVELS, $12.95 each

D-141   **ALL HEROES ARE HATED** by Milton Lesser
AND THE STARS REMAIN by Bryan Berry

D-142   **LAST CALL FOR DOOMSDAY** by Edmond Hamilton
HUNTRESS OF AKKAN by Robert Moore Williams

D-143   **THE MOON PIRATES** by Neil R. Jones
CALLISTO AT WAR by Harl Vincent

D-144   **THUNDER IN THE DAWN** by Henry Kuttner
THE UNCANNY EXPERIMENTS OF DR. VARSAG by David V. Reed

D-145   **A PATTERN FOR MONSTERS** by Randall Garrett
STAR SURGEON by Alan E Nourse

D-146   **THE ATOM CURTAIN** by Nick Boddie Williams
WARLOCK OF SHARRADOR by Gardner F. Fox

D-148   **SECRET OF THE LOST PLANET** by David Wright O'Brien
TELEVISION HILL by George McLociard

D-147   **INTO THE GREEN PRISM** by A Hyatt Verrill
WANDERERS OF THE WOLF-MOON by Nelson S. Bond

D-149   **MINIONS OF THE TIGER** by Chester S. Geier
FOUNDING FATHER by J. F. Bone

D-150   **THE INVISIBLE MAN** by H. G. Wells
THE ISLAND OF DR. MOREAU by H. G. Wells

ARMCHAIR SCIENCE FICTION CLASSICS, $12.95 each

C-61   **THE SHAVER MYSTERY, Book Six**
by Richard. S. Shaver

C-62   **CADUCEUS WILD**
by Ward Moore & Robert Bradford

ARMCHAIR MYSTERY-CRIME DOUBLE NOVELS, $12.95 each

B-1   **THE DEADLY PICK-UP** by Milton Ozaki
KILLER TAKE ALL by James O. Causey

B-2   **THE VIOLENT ONES** by E. Howard Hunt
HIGH HEEL HOMICIDE by Frederick C. Davis

B-3   **FURY ON SUNDAY** by Richard Matheson
THE AGONY COLUMN by Earl Derr Biggers

AN INNOCENT MEAL THAT LED TO A MURDER MYSTERY

In this classic thriller by the man who gave us Charlie Chan, a young American visiting London, Geoffrey West, comes to a posh London hotel for breakfast. During his meal, West innocently checks the personal ads in the London Daily Mail's "Agony Column," which feature all sorts of over-the-top romantic correspondences. His breakfast is interrupted by the arrival of a beautiful American girl and her father, who are seated a few feet away from his table. He notices that the girl is also engrossed in the same column. Soon West has written a letter to the beautiful American, to be posted in the Agony Column in the hope of catching her eye and serving as the medium for their introduction. As luck will have it, she reads the letter and responds. A series of letters then commence between the two Americans. But before long a maze of perplexing circumstances arise, and soon interwoven into their writings is an all too real murder mystery.

AUTHOR PORTRAIT

Earl Derr Biggers 1884-1933

Harvard graduate Earl Derr Biggers is known by most people as the father of Charlie Chan, writing a plethora of Chan novels in his lifetime. However, Biggers wrote many other fine non-Chan mystery works including the classic 1913 shudder tale, "Seven Keys to Baldpate," which has been made into a motion picture no less than nine times since 1916.

THE AGONY
COLUMN

By
EARL DERR BIGGERS

ARMCHAIR FICTION
PO Box 4369, Medford, Oregon 97504

*For more information about Armchair Books and products, visit our
website at…*

www.armchairfiction.com

Or email us at…

armchairfiction@yahoo.com

CHAPTER ONE

London that historic summer was almost unbearably hot. It seems, looking back, as though the big baking city in those days was meant to serve as an anteroom of torture—an inadequate bit of preparation for the hell that was soon to break in the guise of the Great War. About the soda-water bar in the drug store near the Hotel Cecil many American tourists found solace in the sirups and creams of home. Through the open windows of the Piccadilly tea shops you might catch glimpses of the English consuming quarts of hot tea in order to become cool. It is a paradox they swear by.

About nine o'clock on the morning of Friday, July twenty-fourth, in that memorable year nineteen hundred and fourteen, Geoffrey West left his apartments in Adelphi Terrace and set out for breakfast at the Carlton. He had found the breakfast room of that dignified hotel the coolest in London, and through some miracle, for the season had passed, strawberries might still be had there. As he took his way through the crowded Strand, surrounded on all sides by honest British faces wet with honest British perspiration he thought longingly of his rooms in Washington Square, New York. For West, despite the English sound of that Geoffrey, was as American as Kansas, his native state, and only pressing business was at that moment holding him in England, far from the country that glowed unusually rosy because of its remoteness.

At the Carlton news stand West bought two morning papers—the Times for study and the Mail for entertainment and then passed on into the restaurant. His waiter—a tall soldierly Prussian, more blond than West himself—saw him coming and, with a nod and a mechanical German smile, set out for the plate of strawberries which he knew would be the first thing desired by the American. West seated himself at his usual table and, spreading out the Daily Mail, sought his favorite column. The first item in that column brought a delighted smile to his face:

"The one who calls me Dearest is not genuine or they would write to me."

Anyone at all familiar with English journalism will recognize at once what department it was that appealed most to West. During his three weeks in London he had been following, with the keenest joy, the daily grist of Personal Notices in the Mail. This string of intimate messages, popularly known as the Agony Column, has long been an honored institution in the English press. In the days of Sherlock Holmes it was in the Times that it flourished, and many a criminal was tracked to earth after he had inserted some alluring mysterious message in it. Later the Telegraph gave it room; but, with the advent of halfpenny journalism, the simple souls moved en masse to the Mail.

Tragedy and comedy mingle in the Agony Column. Erring ones are urged to return for forgiveness; unwelcome suitors are warned that "Father has warrant prepared; fly, Dearest One!" Loves that would shame by their ardor Abelard and Heloise are frankly published—at ten cents a word—for all the town to smile at. The gentleman in the brown derby states with fervor that the blonde governess who got off the tram at Shepherd's Bush has quite won his heart. Will she permit his addresses? Answer; this department. For three weeks West had found this sort of thing delicious reading. Best of all, he could detect in these messages nothing that was not open and innocent. At their worst they were merely an effort to side-step old Lady Convention; this inclination was so rare in the British, he felt it should be encouraged. Besides, he was inordinately fond of mystery and romance, and these engaging twins hovered always about that column.

So, while waiting for his strawberries, he smiled over the ungrammatical outburst of the young lady who had come to doubt the genuineness of him who called her Dearest. He passed on to the second item of the morning. Spoke one whose heart had been completely conquered:

MY LADY sleeps. She of raven tresses. Corner seat from Victoria, Wednesday night. Carried program. Gentleman answering inquiry desires acquaintance. Reply here. —LE ROI.

West made a mental note to watch for the reply of raven tresses. The next message proved to be one of Aye's lyrics—now almost a daily feature of the column:

DEAREST: Tender loving wishes to my dear one. Only to be with you now and always. None "fairer in my eyes." Your name is music to me. I love you more than life itself, my own beautiful darling, my proud sweetheart, my joy, my all! Jealous of everybody. Kiss your dear hands for me. Love you only. Thine ever. —AYE.

Which, reflected West, was generous of Aye—at ten cents a word—and in striking contrast to the penurious lover who wrote, farther along in the column:

—*loveu dearly; wantocu; longing; missu*—

But those extremely personal notices ran not alone to love. Mystery, too, was present, especially in the aquatic utterance:

DEFIANT MERMAID: Not mine. Alligators bitingu now. 'Tis well; delighted. —FIRST FISH.

And the rather sanguinary suggestion:

DE Box: First round; tooth gone. Finale. You will FORGET ME NOT.

At this point West's strawberries arrived and even the Agony Column could not hold his interest. When the last red berry was eaten he turned back to read:

WATERLOO: Wed. 11:53 train. Lady who left in taxi and waved, care to know gent, gray coat? —SINCERE.

Also the more dignified request put forward in:

GREAT CENTRAL: Gentleman who saw lady in bonnet 9 Monday morning in Great Central Hotel lift would greatly value opportunity of obtaining introduction.

This exhausted the joys of the Agony Column for the day, and West, like the solid citizen he really was, took up the Times to discover what might be the morning's news. A great deal of space was given to the appointment of a new principal for Dulwich College. The affairs of the heart, in which that charming creature, Gabrielle Ray, was at the moment involved, likewise claimed attention. And in a quite unimportant corner, in a most unimportant manner, it was related that Austria had sent an ultimatum to Serbia. West had read part way through this stupid little piece of news, when suddenly the Thunderer and all its works became an uninteresting blur.

A girl stood just inside the door of the Carlton breakfast room.

Yes; he should have pondered that despatch from Vienna. But such a girl! It adds nothing at all to say that her hair was a dull sort of gold; her eyes violet. Many girls have been similarly blessed. It was her manner; the sweet way she looked with those violet eyes through a battalion of head waiters and resplendent managers; her air of being at home here in the Carlton or anywhere else that fate might drop her down. Unquestionably she came from oversea—from the States.

She stepped forward into the restaurant. And now slipped also into view, as part of the background for her, a middle-aged man, who wore the conventional black of the statesman. He, too, bore the American label unmistakably. Nearer and nearer to West she drew, and he saw that in her hand she carried a copy of the Daily Mail.

West's waiter was a master of the art of suggesting that no table in the room was worth sitting at save that at which he held ready a chair. Thus he lured the girl and her companion to repose not five feet from where West sat. This accomplished, he whipped out his order book, and stood with pencil poised, like a reporter in an American play.

"The strawberries are delicious," he said in honeyed tones.

The man looked at the girl, a question in his eyes.

"Not for me, dad," she said. "I hate them! Grapefruit, please."

come a breeze to fan the hot cheek of London. It gently stirred his curtains; rustled the papers on his desk.

He considered. Should he at once make known the eminently respectable person he was, the hopelessly respectable people he knew? Hardly! For then, on the instant, like a bubble bursting, would go for good all mystery and romance, and the lady of the grapefruit would lose all interest and listen to him no more. He spoke solemnly to his rustling curtains.

"No," he said. "We must have mystery and romance. But where—where shall we find them?"

On the floor above he heard the solid tramp of military boots belonging to his neighbor, Captain Stephen Fraser-Freer, of the Twelfth Cavalry, Indian Army, home on furlough from that colony beyond the seas. It was from that room overhead that romance and mystery were to come in mighty store; but Geoffrey West little suspected it at the moment. Hardly knowing what to say, but gaining inspiration as he went along, he wrote the first of seven letters to the lady at the Carlton. And the epistle he dropped in the post box at midnight follows here:

DEAR LADY OF THE GRAPEFRUIT: You are very kind. Also, you are wise. Wise, because into my clumsy little Personal you read nothing that was not there. You knew it immediately for what it was—the timid tentative clutch of a shy man at the skirts of Romance in passing. Believe me, old Conservatism was with me when I wrote that message. He was fighting hard. He followed me, struggling, shrieking, protesting, to the post box itself. But I whipped him. Glory be! I did for him.

We are young but once, I told him. After that, what use to signal to Romance? The lady at least, I said, will understand. He sneered at that. He shook his silly gray head. I will admit he had me worried. But now you have justified my faith in you. Thank you a million times for that!

Three weeks I have been in this huge, ungainly, indifferent city, longing for the States. Three weeks the Agony Column has been my sole diversion. And then—through the doorway of the Carlton restaurant—you came—

It is of myself that I must write, I know. I will not, then, tell you what is in my mind—the picture of you I carry. It would mean little to you. Many Texan gallants, no doubt, have told you the same while the moon was bright above you and the breeze was softly whispering through the branches of—the branches of the—of the—

Confound it, I don't know! I have never been in Texas. It is a vice in me I hope soon to correct. All day I intended to look up Texas in the encyclopedia. But all day I have dwelt in the clouds. And there are no reference books in the clouds.

Now I am down to earth in my quiet study. Pens, ink and paper are before me. I must prove myself a person worth knowing.

From his rooms, they say, you can tell much about a man. But, alas! these peaceful rooms in Adelphi Terrace—I shall not tell the number—were sublet furnished. So if you could see me now you would be judging me by the possessions left behind by one Anthony Bartholomew. There is much dust on them. Judge neither Anthony nor me by that. Judge rather Walters, the caretaker, who lives in the basement with his gray-haired wife. Walters was a gardener once, and his whole life is wrapped up in the courtyard on which my balcony looks down. There he spends his time, while up above the dust gathers in the corners—

Does this picture distress you, my lady? You should see the courtyard! You would not blame Walters then. It is a sample of Paradise left at our door—that courtyard. As English as a hedge, as neat, as beautiful. London is a roar somewhere beyond; between our court and the great city is a magic gate, forever closed. It was the court that led me to take these rooms.

And, since you are one who loves mystery, I am going to relate to you the odd chain of circumstances that brought me here.

For the first link in that chain we must go back to Interlaken. Have you been there yet? A quiet little town, lying beautiful between two shimmering lakes, with the great Jungfrau itself for scenery. From the dining-room of one lucky hotel you may look up at dinner and watch the old-rose afterglow light the snow-capped mountain. You would not say then of strawberries: "I hate them." Or of anything else in all the world.

A month ago I was in Interlaken. One evening after dinner I strolled along the main street, where all the hotels and shops are drawn up at attention before the lovely mountain. In front of one of the shops I saw a collection of walking sticks and, since I needed one for climbing, I paused to look them over. I had been at this only a moment when a young Englishman stepped up and also began examining the sticks.

I had made a selection from the lot and was turning away to find the shopkeeper, when the Englishman spoke. He was lean, distinguished-looking, though quite young, and had that well-tubbed appearance which I am convinced is the great factor that has enabled the English to assert their authority over colonies like Egypt and India, where men are not so thoroughly bathed.

"Er—if you'll pardon me, old chap," he said. "Not that stick—if you don't mind my saying so. It's not tough enough for mountain work. I would suggest—"

To say that I was astonished is putting it mildly. If you know the English at all, you know it is not their habit to address strangers, even under the most pressing circumstances. Yet here was one of that haughty race actually interfering in my selection of a stick. I ended by buying the one he preferred, and he strolled along with me in the direction of my hotel, chatting meantime in a fashion far from British.

We stopped at the Kursaal, where we listened to the music, had a drink and threw away a few francs on the little horses. He came with me to the veranda of my hotel. I was surprised, when he took his leave, to find that he regarded me in the light of an old friend. He said he would call on me the next morning.

I made up my mind that Archibald Enwright—for that, he told me, was his name—was an adventurer down on his luck, who chose to forget his British exclusiveness under the stern necessity of getting money somehow, somewhere. The next day, I decided, I should be the victim of a touch.

But my prediction failed; Enwright seemed to have plenty of money. On that first evening I had mentioned to him that I expected shortly to be in London, and he often referred to the fact. As the time approached for me to leave Interlaken he began to throw out the suggestion that he should like to have me meet some of his people in England. This, also, was unheard of—against all precedent.

Nevertheless, when I said good-by to him he pressed into my hand a letter of introduction to his cousin, Captain Stephen Fraser-Freer, of the Twelfth Cavalry, Indian Army, who, he said, would be glad to make me at home in London, where he was on furlough at the time—or would be when I reached there.

"Stephen's a good sort," said Enwright. "He'll be jolly pleased to show you the ropes. Give him my best, old boy!"

Of course I took the letter. But I puzzled greatly over the affair. What could be the meaning of this sudden warm attachment that Archie had formed for me? Why should he want to pass me along to his cousin at a time when that gentleman, back home after two years in India, would be, no doubt, extremely busy? I made up my mind I would not present the letter, despite the fact that Archie had with great persistence wrung from me a promise to do so. I had met many English gentlemen, and I felt they were not the sort—despite the example of Archie—to take a wandering American to their bosoms when he came with a mere letter. By easy stages I came on to London. Here I met a friend, just sailing for home, who told me of some sad experiences he had had with letters of introduction—of the cold, fishy, "My-dear-fellow-why-trouble-me-with-it?" stares that had greeted their presentation. Good-hearted men all, he said, but averse to strangers; an ever-present trait in the English—always excepting Archie.

So I put the letter to Captain Fraser-Freer out of my mind. I had business acquaintances here and a few English friends, and I found these, as always, courteous and charming. But it is to my advantage to meet as many people as may be, and after drifting about for a week I set out one afternoon to call on my captain. I told myself that here was an Englishman who had perhaps thawed a bit in the great oven of India. If not, no harm would be done.

It was then that I came for the first time to this house on Adelphi Terrace, for it was the address Archie had given me. Walters let me in, and I learned from him that Captain Fraser-Freer had not yet arrived from India. His rooms were ready—he had kept them during his absence, as seems to be the custom over here—and he was expected soon. Perhaps—said Walters—his wife remembered the date. He left me in the lower hall while he went to ask her.

Waiting, I strolled to the rear of the hall. And then, through an open window that let in the summer, I saw for the first time that courtyard which is my great love in London—the old ivy-covered walls of brick; the neat paths between the blooming beds; the rustic seat; the magic gate. It was incredible that just outside lay the world's biggest city, with all its poverty and wealth, its sorrows and joys, its roar and rattle. Here was a garden for Jane Austen to people with fine ladies and courtly gentlemen—here was a garden to dream in, to adore and to cherish.

When Walters came back to tell me that his wife was uncertain as to the exact date when the captain would return, I began to rave about that courtyard. At once he was my friend. I had been looking for quiet lodgings away from the hotel, and I was delighted to find that on the second floor, directly under the captain's rooms, there was a suite to be sublet.

Walters gave me the address of the agents; and, after submitting to an examination that could not have been more severe if I had asked for the hand of the senior partner's daughter, they let me come here to live. The garden was mine!

And the captain? Three days after I arrived I heard above me, for the first time, the tread of his military boots. Now again my courage began to fail. I should have preferred to leave Archie's letter lying in my desk and know my neighbor only by his tread above me. I felt that perhaps I had been presumptuous in coming to live in the same house with him. But I had represented myself to Walters as an acquaintance of the captain's and the caretaker had lost no time in telling me that "my friend" was safely home.

So one night, a week ago, I got up my nerve and went to the captain's rooms. I knocked. He called to me to enter and I stood in his study, facing him. He was a tall handsome man, fair-haired, mustached—the very figure that you, my lady, in your boarding-school days, would have wished him to be. His manner, I am bound to admit, was not cordial.

"Captain," I began, "I am very sorry to intrude—" It wasn't the thing to say, of course, but I was fussed. "However, I happen to be a neighbor of yours, and I have here a letter of introduction from your cousin, Archibald Enwright. I met him in Interlaken and we became very good friends."

"Indeed!" said the captain.

He held out his hand for the letter, as though it were evidence at a court-martial. I passed it over, wishing I hadn't come. He read it through. It was a long letter, considering its nature. While I waited, standing by his desk—he hadn't asked me to sit down—I looked about the room. It was much like my own study, only I think a little dustier. Being on the third floor it was farther from the garden, consequently Walters reached there seldom.

The captain turned back and began to read the letter again. This was decidedly embarrassing. Glancing down, I happened to see on his desk an odd knife, which I fancy he had brought from India. The blade was of steel, dangerously sharp, the hilt of gold, carved to represent some heathen figure.

Then the captain looked up from Archie's letter and his cold gaze fell full upon me.

"My dear fellow," he said, "to the best of my knowledge, I have no cousin named Archibald Enwright."

A pleasant situation, you must admit! It's bad enough when you come to them with a letter from their mother, but here was I in this Englishman's rooms, boldly flaunting in his face a warm note of commendation from a cousin who did not exist!

"I owe you an apology," I said. I tried to be as haughty as he, and fell short by about two miles. "I brought the letter in good faith."

"No doubt of that," he answered.

"Evidently it was given me by some adventurer for purposes of his own," I went on; "though I am at a loss to guess what they could have been."

"I'm frightfully sorry—really," said he. But he said it with the London inflection, which plainly implies: "I'm nothing of the sort."

A painful pause. I felt that he ought to give me back the letter; but he made no move to do so. And, of course, I didn't ask for it.

"Ah—er—good night," said I and hurried toward the door.

"Good night," he answered, and I left him standing there with Archie's accursed letter in his hand.

That is the story of how I came to this house in Adelphi Terrace. There is mystery in it, you must admit, my lady. Once or twice since that uncomfortable call I have passed the captain on the stairs; but the halls are very dark, and for that I am grateful. I hear him often above me; in fact, I hear him as I write this.

Who was Archie? What was the idea? I wonder.

Ah, well, I have my garden, and for that I am indebted to Archie the garrulous. It is nearly midnight now. The roar of London has died away to a fretful murmur, and somehow across this baking town a breeze has found its way. It whispers over the green grass, in the ivy that climbs my wall, in the soft murky folds of my curtains. Whispers—what?

Whispers, perhaps, the dreams that go with this, the first of my letters to you. They are dreams that even I dare not whisper yet.

And so—good night.

THE STRAWBERRY MAN.

CHAPTER THREE

With a smile that betrayed unusual interest, the daughter of the Texas statesman read that letter on Thursday morning in her room at the Carlton. There was no question about it—the first epistle from the strawberry-mad one had caught and held her attention. All day, as she dragged her father through picture galleries, she found herself looking forward to another morning, wondering, eager.

But on the following morning Sadie Haight, the maid through whom this odd correspondence was passing, had no letter to deliver. The news rather disappointed the daughter of Texas. At noon she insisted on returning to the hotel for luncheon, though, as her father pointed out, they were far from the Carlton at the time. Her journey was rewarded. Letter number two was waiting; and as she read she gasped.

DEAR LADY AT THE CARLTON: I am writing this at three in the morning, with London silent as the grave, beyond our garden. That I am so late in getting to it is not because I did not think of you all day yesterday; not because I did not sit down at my desk at seven last evening to address you. Believe me, only the most startling, the most appalling accident could have held me up.

That most startling, most appalling accident has happened.

I am tempted to give you the news at once in one striking and terrible sentence. And I could write that sentence. A tragedy, wrapped in mystery as impenetrable as a London fog, has befallen our quiet little house in Adelphi Terrace. In their basement room the Walters family, sleepless, overwhelmed, sit silent; on the dark stairs outside my door I hear at intervals the tramp of men on unhappy missions—But no; I must go back to the very start of it all:

153

Last night I had an early dinner at Simpson's, in the Strand—so early that I was practically alone in the restaurant. The letter I was about to write to you was uppermost in my mind and, having quickly dined, I hurried back to my rooms. I remember clearly that, as I stood in the street before our house fumbling for my keys, Big Ben on the Parliament Buildings struck the hour of seven. The chime of the great bell rang out in our peaceful thoroughfare like a loud and friendly greeting.

Gaining my study, I sat down at once to write. Over my head I could hear Captain Fraser-Freer moving about—attiring himself, probably, for dinner. I was thinking, with an amused smile, how horrified he would be if he knew that the crude American below him had dined at the impossible hour of six, when suddenly I heard, in that room above me, some stranger talking in a harsh determined tone. Then came the captain's answering voice, calmer, more dignified. This conversation went along for some time, growing each moment more excited. Though I could not distinguish a word of it, I had the uncomfortable feeling that there was a controversy on; and I remember feeling annoyed that anyone should thus interfere with my composition of your letter, which I regarded as most important, you may be sure.

At the end of five minutes of argument there came the heavy thump-thump of men struggling above me. It recalled my college days, when we used to hear the fellows in the room above us throwing each other about in an excess of youth and high spirits. But this seemed more grim, more determined, and I did not like it.—However, I reflected that it was none of my business. I tried to think about my letter.

The struggle ended with a particularly heavy thud that shook our ancient house to its foundations. I sat listening, somehow very much depressed. There was no sound. It was not entirely dark outside—the long twilight—and the frugal Walters had not lighted the hall lamps. Somebody was coming down the stairs very quietly—but their creaking betrayed him. I waited for him to pass through the shaft of light that poured from the door open at my back. At that moment Fate intervened in the shape of a breeze through my windows, the door banged shut, and a heavy man rushed by me in the darkness and ran down the stairs. I knew he was heavy, because the passageway was narrow and he had to push me aside to get by. I heard him swear beneath his breath.

Quickly I went to a hall window at the far end that looked out on the street. But the front door did not open; no one came out. I was puzzled for a second; then I reentered my room and hurried to my balcony. I could make out the dim figure of a man running through the garden at the rear—that garden of which I have so often spoken. He did not try to open the gate; he climbed it, and so disappeared from sight into the alley.

For a moment I considered. These were odd actions, surely; but was it my place to interfere? I remembered the cold stare in the eyes of Captain Fraser-Freer when I presented that letter. I saw him standing motionless in his murky study, as amiable as a statue. Would he welcome an intrusion from me now?

Finally I made up my mind to forget these things and went down to find Walters. He and his wife were eating their dinner in the basement. I told him what had happened. He said he had let no visitor in to see the captain, and was inclined to view my misgivings with a cold British eye. However, I persuaded him to go with me to the captain's rooms.

The captain's door was open. Remembering that in England the way of the intruder is hard, I ordered Walters to go first. He stepped into the room, where the gas flickered feebly in an aged chandelier.

"My God, sir!" said Walters, a servant even now.

And at last I write that sentence: Captain Fraser-Freer of the Indian Army lay dead on the floor, a smile that was almost a sneer on his handsome English face!

The horror of it is strong with me now as I sit in the silent morning in this room of mine which is so like the one in which the captain died. He had been stabbed just over the heart, and my first thought was of that odd Indian knife which I had seen

lying on his study table. I turned quickly to seek it, but it was
gone. And as I looked at the table it came to me that here in
this dusty room there must be finger prints—many finger prints.

The room was quite in order, despite those sounds of
struggle. One or two odd matters met my eye. On the table
stood a box from a florist in Bond Street. The lid had been
removed and I saw that the box contained a number of white
asters. Beside the box lay a scarf-pin—an emerald scarab. And
not far from the captain's body lay what is known—owing to
the German city where it is made—as a Homburg hat.

I recalled that it is most important at such times that nothing
be disturbed, and I turned to old Walters. His face was like this
paper on which I write; his knees trembled beneath him.

"Walters," said I, "we must leave things just as they are until
the police arrive. Come with me while I notify Scotland Yard."

"Very good, sir," said Walters.

We went down then to the telephone in the lower hall, and I
called up the Yard. I was told that an inspector would come at
once and I went back to my room to wait for him.

You can well imagine the feelings that were mine as I waited.
Before this mystery should be solved, I foresaw that I might be
involved to a degree that was unpleasant if not dangerous.
Walters would remember that I first came here as one
acquainted with the captain. He had noted, I felt sure, the lack
of intimacy between the captain and myself, once the former
arrived from India. He would no doubt testify that I had been
most anxious to obtain lodgings in the same house with Fraser-
Freer. Then there was the matter of my letter from Archie. I
must keep that secret, I felt sure. Lastly, there was not a living
soul to back me up in my story of the quarrel that preceded the
captain's death, of the man who escaped by way of the garden.

Alas, thought I, even the most stupid policeman can not fail
to look upon me with the eye of suspicion!

In about twenty minutes three men arrived from Scotland
Yard. By that time I had worked myself up into a state of
absurd nervousness. I heard Walters let them in; heard them

climb the stairs and walk about in the room overhead. In a short time Walters knocked at my door and told me that Chief Inspector Bray desired to speak to me. As I preceded the servant up the stairs I felt toward him as an accused murderer must feel toward the witness who has it in his power to swear his life away.

He was a big active man—Bray; blond as are so many Englishmen. His every move spoke efficiency. Trying to act as unconcerned as an innocent man should—but failing miserably, I fear—I related to him my story of the voices, the struggle, and the heavy man who had got by me in the hall and later climbed our gate. He listened without comment. At the end he said:

"You were acquainted with the captain?"

"Slightly," I told him. Archie's letter kept popping into my mind, frightening me. "I had just met him—that is all; through a friend of his—Archibald Enwright was the name."

"Is Enwright in London to vouch for you?"

"I'm afraid not. I last heard of him in Interlaken."

"Yes? How did you happen to take rooms in this house?"

"The first time I called to see the captain he had not yet arrived from India. I was looking for lodgings and I took a great fancy to the garden here."

It sounded silly, put like that. I wasn't surprised that the inspector eyed me with scorn. But I rather wished he hadn't.

Bray began to walk about the room, ignoring me.

"White asters; scarab pin; Homburg hat," he detailed, pausing before the table where those strange exhibits lay.

A constable came forward carrying newspapers in his hand.

"What is it?" Bray asked.

"The Daily Mail, sir," said the constable. "The issues of July twenty-seventh, twenty-eighth, twenty-ninth and thirtieth."

Bray took the papers in his hand, glanced at them and tossed them contemptuously into a waste-basket. He turned to Walters.

"Sorry, sir," said Walters; "but I was so taken aback! Nothing like this has ever happened to me before. I'll go at once—"

"No," replied Bray sharply. "Never mind. I'll attend to it—"

There was a knock at the door. Bray called "Come!" and a slender boy, frail but with a military bearing, entered.

"Hello, Walters!" he said, smiling. "What's up? I-"

He stopped suddenly as his eyes fell upon the divan where Fraser-Freer lay. In an instant he was at the dead man's side.

"Stephen!" he cried in anguish.

"Who are you?" demanded the inspector—rather rudely, I thought.

"It's the captain's brother, sir," put in Walters. "Lieutenant Norman Fraser-Freer, of the Royal Fusiliers."

There fell a silence.

"A great calamity, sir—" began Walters to the boy.

I have rarely seen anyone so overcome as young Fraser-Freer. Watching him, it seemed to me that the affection existing between him and the man on the divan must have been a beautiful thing. He turned away from his brother at last, and Walters sought to give him some idea of what had happened.

"You will pardon me, gentlemen," said the lieutenant. "This has been a terrible shock! I didn't dream, of course—I just dropped in for a word with—with him. And now—"

We said nothing. We let him apologize, as a true Englishman must, for his public display of emotion.

"I'm sorry," Bray remarked in a moment, his eyes still shifting about the room, "especially as England may soon have great need of men like the captain. Now, gentlemen, I want to say this: I am the Chief of the Special Branch at the Yard. This is no ordinary murder. For reasons I can not disclose—and, I may add, for the best interests of the empire—news of the captain's tragic death must be kept for the present out of the newspapers. I mean, of course, the manner of his going. A mere death notice, you understand—the inference being that it was a natural taking off."

"I understand," said the lieutenant, as one who knows more than he tells.

"Thank you," said Bray. "I shall leave you to attend to the matter, as far as your family is concerned. You will take charge of the body. As for the rest of you, I forbid you to mention this matter outside."

And now Bray stood looking, with a puzzled air, at me.

"You are an American?" he said, and I judged he did not care for Americans.

"I am," I told him.

"Know anyone at your consulate?" he demanded.

Thank heaven, I did! There is an under-secretary there named Watson—I went to college with him. I mentioned him to Bray.

"Very good," said the inspector. "You are free to go. But you must understand that you are an important witness in this case, and if you attempt to leave London you will be locked up."

So I came back to my rooms, horribly entangled in a mystery that is little to my liking. I have been sitting here in my study for some time, going over it again and again. There have been many footsteps on the stairs, many voices in the hall.

Waiting here for the dawn, I have come to be very sorry for the cold handsome captain. After all, he was a man; his very tread on the floor above, which it shall never hear again, told me that.

What does it all mean? Who was the man in the hall, the man who had argued so loudly, who had struck so surely with that queer Indian knife? Where is the knife now?

And, above all, what do the white asters signify? And the scarab scarf-pin? And that absurd Homburg hat?

Lady of the Carlton, you wanted mystery. When I wrote that first letter to you, little did I dream that I should soon have it to give you in overwhelming measure.

And—believe me when I say it—through all this your face has been constantly before me—your face as I saw it that bright morning in the hotel breakfast room. You have forgiven me, I know, for the manner in which I addressed you. I had seen your eyes and the temptation was great—very great.

It is dawn in the garden now and London is beginning to stir. So this time it is—good morning, my lady.

THE STRAWBERRY MAN.

CHAPTER FOUR

It is hardly necessary to intimate that this letter came as something of a shock to the young woman who received it. For the rest of that day the many sights of London held little interest for her—so little, indeed, that her perspiring father began to see visions of his beloved Texas; and once hopefully suggested an early return home. The coolness with which this idea was received plainly showed him that he was on the wrong track; so he sighed and sought solace at the bar.

That night the two from Texas attended His Majesty's Theater, where Bernard Shaw's latest play was being performed; and the witty Irishman would have been annoyed to see the scant attention one lovely young American in the audience gave his lines. The American in question retired at midnight, with eager thoughts turned toward the morning.

And she was not disappointed. When her maid, a stolid Englishwoman, appeared at her bedside early Saturday she carried a letter, which she handed over, with the turned-up nose of one who aids but does not approve. Quickly the girl tore it open.

DEAR Texas LADY: I am writing this late in the afternoon. The sun is casting long black shadows on the garden lawn, and the whole world is so bright and matter-of-fact I have to argue with myself to be convinced that the events of that tragic night through which I passed really happened.

The newspapers this morning helped to make it all seem a dream; not a line—not a word, that I can find. When I think of America, and how by this time the reporters would be swarming through our house if this thing had happened over there, I am the more astonished. But then, I know these English papers. The great Joe Chamberlain died the other night at ten, and it

161

was noon the next day when the first paper to carry the story appeared—screaming loudly that it had scored a beat. It had. Other lands, other methods.

It was probably not difficult for Bray to keep journalists such as these in the dark. So their great ungainly sheets come out in total ignorance of a remarkable story in Adelphi Terrace. Famished for real news, they begin to hint at a huge war cloud on the horizon. Because tottering Austria has declared war on tiny Serbia, because the Kaiser is today hurrying, with his best dramatic effect, home to Berlin, they see all Europe shortly bathed in blood. A nightmare born of torrid days and tossing nights!

But it is of the affair in Adelphi Terrace that you no doubt want to hear. One sequel of the tragedy, which adds immeasurably to the mystery of it all, has occurred, and I alone am responsible for its discovery. But to go back:

I returned from mailing your letter at dawn this morning, very tired from the tension of the night. I went to bed, but could not sleep. More and more it was preying on my mind that I was in a most unhappy position. I had not liked the looks cast at me by Inspector Bray, or his voice when he asked how I came to live in this house. I told myself I should not be safe until the real murderer of the poor captain was found; and so I began to puzzle over the few clues in the case—especially over the asters, the scarab pin and the Homburg hat.

It was then I remembered the four copies of the Daily Mail that Bray had casually thrown into the waste-basket as of no interest. I had glanced over his shoulder as he examined these papers, and had seen that each of them was folded so that our favorite department—the Agony Column—was uppermost. It happened I had in my desk copies of the Mail for the past week. You will understand why.

I rose, found those papers, and began to read. It was then that I made the astounding discovery to which I have alluded.

For a time after making it I was dumb with amazement, so that no course of action came readily to mind. In the end I decided that the thing for me to do was to wait for Bray's return in the morning and then point out to him the error he had made in ignoring the Mail.

Bray came in about eight o'clock and a few minutes later I heard another man ascend the stairs. I was shaving at the time, but I quickly completed the operation and, slipping on a bathrobe, hurried up to the captain's rooms. The younger brother had seen to the removal of the unfortunate man's body in the night, and, aside from Bray and the stranger who had arrived almost simultaneously with him, there was no one but a sleepy-eyed constable there.

Bray's greeting was decidedly grouchy. The stranger, however—a tall bronzed man—made himself known to me in the most cordial manner. He told me he was Colonel Hughes, a close friend of the dead man; and that, unutterably shocked and grieved, he had come to inquire whether there was anything he might do. "Inspector," said I, "last night in this room you held in your hand four copies of the Daily Mail. You tossed them into that basket as of no account. May I suggest that you rescue those copies, as I have a rather startling matter to make clear to you?" Too grand an official to stoop to a waste-basket, he nodded to the constable. The latter brought the papers; and, selecting one from the lot, I spread it out on the table. "The issue of July twenty-seventh," I said.

I pointed to an item half-way down the column of Personal Notices. You yourself, my lady, may read it there if you happen to have saved a copy. It ran as follows:

"RANGOON: The asters are in full bloom in the garden at Canterbury. They are very beautiful—especially the white ones."

Bray grunted, and opened his little eyes. I took up the issue of the following day—the twenty-eighth:

"RANGOON: We have been forced to sell father's stick-pin—the emerald scarab he brought home from Cairo."

I had Bray's interest now. He leaned heavily toward me, puffing. Greatly excited, I held before his eyes the issue of the twenty-ninth:

"RANGOON: Homburg hat gone forever—caught by a breeze—into the river."

"And finally," said I to the inspector, "the last message of all, in the issue of the thirtieth of July—on sale in the streets some twelve hours before Fraser-Freer was murdered. See!"

"RANGOON: To-night at ten. Regent Street. —Y.O.G."

Bray was silent.

"I take it you are aware, Inspector," I said, "that for the past two years Captain Fraser-Freer was stationed at Rangoon."

Still he said nothing; just looked at me with those foxy little eyes that I was coming to detest. At last he spoke sharply:

"Just how," he demanded, "did you happen to discover those messages? You were not in this room last night after I left?" He turned angrily to the constable. "I gave orders—"

"No," I put in; "I was not in this room. I happened to have on file in my rooms copies of the Mail, and by the merest chance—"

I saw that I had blundered. Undoubtedly my discovery of those messages was too pat. Once again suspicion looked my way.

"Thank you very much," said Bray. "I'll keep this in mind."

"Have you communicated with my friend at the consulate?" I asked.

"Yes. That's all. Good morning."

So I went.

I had been back in my room some twenty minutes when there came a knock on the door, and Colonel Hughes entered. He was a genial man, in the early forties I should say, tanned by some sun not English, and gray at the temples.

"My dear sir," he said without preamble, "this is a most appalling business!"

"Decidedly," I answered. "Will you sit down?"

"Thank you." He sat and gazed frankly into my eyes. "Policemen," he added meaningly, "are a most suspicious tribe—often without reason. I am sorry you happen to be involved in this affair, for I may say that I fancy you to be exactly what you seem. May I add that, if you should ever need a friend, I am at your service?"

I was touched; I thanked him as best I could. His tone was so sympathetic and before I realized it I was telling him the whole story—of Archie and his letter; of my falling in love with a garden; of the startling discovery that the captain had never heard of his cousin; and of my subsequent unpleasant position. He leaned back in his chair and closed his eyes.

"I suppose," he said, "that no man ever carries an unsealed letter of introduction without opening it to read just what praises have been lavished upon him. It is human nature—I have done it often. May I make so bold as to inquire—"

"Yes," said I. "It was unsealed and I did read it. Considering its purpose, it struck me as rather long. There were many warm words for me—words beyond all reason in view of my brief acquaintance with Enwright. I also recall that he mentioned how long he had been in Interlaken, and that he said he expected to reach London about the first of August."

"The first of August," repeated the colonel. "That is to-morrow. Now—if you'll be so kind—just what happened last night?"

Again I ran over the events of that tragic evening—the quarrel; the heavy figure in the hall; the escape by way of the seldom-used gate.

"My boy," said Colonel Hughes as he rose to go, "the threads of this tragedy stretch far—some of them to India; some to a country I will not name. I may say frankly that I have other and greater interest in the matter than that of the captain's friend. For the present that is in strict confidence between us; the police are well-meaning, but they sometimes blunder. Did I understand you to say that you have copies of the Mail containing those odd messages?"

"Right here in my desk," said I. I got them for him.

"I think I shall take them—if I may," he said. "You will, of course, not mention this little visit of mine. We shall meet again. Good morning."

And he went away, carrying those papers with their strange signals to Rangoon.

Somehow I feel wonderfully cheered by his call. For the first time since seven last evening I begin to breathe freely again.

And so, lady who likes mystery, the matter stands on the afternoon of the last day of July, nineteen hundred and fourteen.

I shall mail you this letter to-night. It is my third to you, and it carries with it three times the dreams that went with the first; for they are dreams that live not only at night, when the moon is on the courtyard, but also in the bright light of day.

Yes—I am remarkably cheered. I realize that I have not eaten at all—save a cup of coffee from the trembling hand of Walters—since last night, at Simpson's. I am going now to dine. I shall begin with grapefruit. I realize that I am suddenly very fond of grapefruit.

How bromidic to note it—we have many tastes in common! EX-STRAWBERRY MAN.

The third letter from her correspondent of the Agony Column increased in the mind of the lovely young woman at the Carlton the excitement and tension the second had created. For a long time, on the Saturday morning of its receipt, she sat in her room puzzling over the mystery of the house in Adelphi Terrace. When first she had heard that Captain Fraser-Freer, of the Indian Army, was dead of a knife wound over the heart, the news had shocked her like that of the loss of some old and dear friend. She had desired passionately the apprehension of his murderer, and had turned over and over in her mind the possibilities of white asters, a scarab pin and a Homburg hat.

Perhaps the girl longed for the arrest of the guilty man thus keenly because this jaunty young friend of hers—a friend whose name she did not know—to whom, indeed, she had never spoken—was so dangerously entangled in the affair. For, from what she knew of Geoffrey West, from her casual glance in the restaurant and, far more, from his letters, she liked him extremely.

And now came his third letter, in which he related the connection of that hat, that pin and those asters with the column in the Mail which had first brought them together. As it happened, she, too, had copies of the paper for the first four days of the week. She went to her sitting-room, unearthed these copies, and—gasped! For from the column in Monday's paper stared up at her the cryptic words to Rangoon concerning asters in a garden at Canterbury. In the other three issues as well, she found the identical messages her strawberry man had quoted. She sat for a moment in deep thought; sat, in fact, until at her door came the enraged knocking of a hungry parent who had been waiting a full hour in the lobby below for her to join him at breakfast.

"Come, come!" boomed her father, entering at her invitation. "Don't sit here all day mooning. I'm hungry if you're not."

With quick apologies she made ready to accompany him down-stairs. Firmly, as she planned their campaign for the day, she resolved to put from her mind all thought of Adelphi Terrace. How well she succeeded may be judged from a speech made by her father that night just before dinner:

"Have you lost your tongue, Marian? You're as uncommunicative as a newly-elected office-holder. If you can't get a little more life into these expeditions of ours we'll pack up and head for home."

She smiled, patted his shoulder and promised to improve. But he appeared to be in a gloomy mood.

"I believe we ought to go, anyhow," he went on. "In my opinion this war is going to spread like a prairie fire. The Kaiser got back to Berlin yesterday. He'll sign the mobilization orders today as sure as fate. For the past week, on the Berlin Bourse, Canadian Pacific stock has been dropping. That means they expect England to come in."

He gazed darkly into the future. It may seem that, for an American statesman, he had an unusual grasp of European politics. This is easily explained by the fact that he had been talking with the bootblack at the Carlton Hotel.

"Yes," he said with sudden decision, "I'll go down to the steamship offices early Monday morning."

CHAPTER FIVE

His daughter heard these words with a sinking heart. She had a most unhappy picture of herself boarding a ship and sailing out of Liverpool or Southampton, leaving the mystery that so engrossed her thoughts forever unsolved. Wisely she diverted her father's thoughts toward the question of food. She had heard, she said, that Simpson's, in the Strand, was an excellent place to dine. They would go there, and walk. She suggested a short detour that would carry them through Adelphi Terrace. It seemed she had always wanted to see Adelphi Terrace.

As they passed through that silent Street she sought to guess, from an inspection of the grim forbidding house fronts, back of which lay the lovely garden, the romantic mystery. But the houses were so very much like one another. Before one of them, she noted, a taxi waited.

After dinner her father pleaded for a music-hall as against what he called "some highfaluting, teacup English play." He won. Late that night, as they rode back to the Carlton, special editions were being proclaimed in the streets. Germany was mobilizing!

The girl from Texas retired, wondering what epistolary surprise the morning would bring forth. It brought forth this:

DEAR DAUGHTER OF THE SENATE: Or is it Congress? I could not quite decide. But surely in one or the other of those august bodies your father sits when he is not at home in Texas or viewing Europe through his daughter's eyes. One look at him and I had gathered that.

But Washington is far from London, isn't it? And it is London that interests us most—though father's constituents must not know that. It is really a wonderful, an astounding city,

169

once you have got the feel of the tourist out of your soul. I have been reading the most enthralling essays on it, written by a newspaper man who first fell desperately in love with it at seven—an age when the whole glittering town was symbolized for him by the fried-fish shop at the corner of the High Street. With him I have been going through its gray and furtive thoroughfares in the dead of night, and sometimes we have kicked an ash-barrel and sometimes a romance. Some day I might show that London to you—guarding you, of course, from the ash-barrels, if you are that kind. On second thoughts, you aren't. But I know that it is of Adelphi Terrace and a late captain in the Indian Army that you want to hear now. Yesterday, after my discovery of those messages in the Mail and the call of Captain Hughes, passed without incident. Last night I mailed you my third letter, and after wandering for a time amid the alternate glare and gloom of the city, I went back to my rooms and smoked on my balcony while about me the inmates of six million homes sweltered in the heat. Nothing happened. I felt a bit disappointed, a bit cheated, as one might feel on the first night spent at home after many successive visits to exciting plays. Today, the first of August dawned, and still all was quiet. Indeed, it was not until this evening that further developments in the sudden death of Captain Fraser-Freer arrived to disturb me. These developments are strange ones surely, and I shall hasten to relate them.

I dined to-night at a little place in Soho. My waiter was Italian, and on him I amused myself with the Italian in Ten Lessons of which I am foolishly proud. We talked of Fiesole, where he had lived. Once I rode from Fiesole down the hill to Florence in the moonlight. I remember endless walls on which hung roses, fresh and blooming. I remember a gaunt nunnery and two-gray-robed sisters clanging shut the gates. I remember the searchlight from the military encampment, playing constantly over the Arno and the roofs—the eye of Mars that, here in Europe, never closes. And always the flowers nodding above me, stooping now and then to brush my face. I came to think that at the end Paradise, and not a second-rate hotel, was waiting. One may still take that ride, I fancy. Some day—some day—

I dined in Soho. I came back to Adelphi Terrace in the hot, reeking August dusk, reflecting that the mystery in which I was involved was, after a fashion, standing still. In front of our house I noticed a taxi waiting. I thought nothing of it as I entered the murky hallway and climbed the familiar stairs.

My door stood open. It was dark in my study, save for the reflection of the lights of London outside. As I crossed the threshold there came to my nostrils the faint sweet perfume of lilacs. There are no lilacs in our garden, and if there were it is not the season. No, this perfume had been brought there by a woman—a woman who sat at my desk and raised her head as I entered.

"You will pardon this intrusion," she said in the correct careful English of one who has learned the speech from a book. "I have come for a brief word with you—then I shall go."

I could think of nothing to say. I stood gaping like a schoolboy.

"My word," the woman went on, "is in the nature of advice. We do not always like those who give us advice. None the less, I trust that you will listen."

I found my tongue then.

"I am listening," I said stupidly. "But first—a light—" And I moved toward the matches on the mantelpiece.

Quickly the woman rose and faced me. I saw then that she wore a veil—not a heavy veil, but a fluffy, attractive thing that was yet sufficient to screen her features from me.

"I beg of you," she cried, "no light!" And as I paused, undecided, she added, in a tone which suggested lips that pout: "It is such a little thing to ask—surely you will not refuse."

I suppose I should have insisted. But her voice was charming, her manner perfect, and that odor of lilacs reminiscent of a garden I knew long ago, at home.

"Very well," said I.

"Oh—I am grateful to you," she answered. Her tone changed. "I understand that, shortly after seven o'clock last Thursday evening, you heard in the room above you the sounds of a struggle. Such has been your testimony to the police?"

"It has," said I.

"Are you quite certain as to the hour?" I felt that she was smiling at me. "Might it not have been later—or earlier?"

"I am sure it was just after seven," I replied. "I'll tell you why: I had just returned from dinner and while I was unlocking the door Big Ben on the House of Parliament struck—"

She raised her hand.

"No matter," she said, and there was a touch of iron in her voice. "You are no longer sure of that. Thinking it over, you have come to the conclusion that it may have been barely six-thirty when you heard the noise of a struggle."

"Indeed?" said I. I tried to sound sarcastic, but I was really too astonished by her tone.

"Yes—indeed!" she replied. "That is what you will tell Inspector Bray when next you see him. 'It may have been six-thirty,' you will tell him. 'I have thought it over and I am not certain.' "

"Even for a very charming lady," I said "I can not misrepresent the facts in a matter so important. It was after seven—"

"I am not asking you to do a favor for a lady," she replied. "I am asking you to do a favor for yourself. If you refuse the consequences may be most unpleasant."

"I'm rather at a loss—" I began.

She was silent for a moment. Then she turned and I felt her looking at me through the veil.

"Who was Archibald Enwright?" she demanded. My heart sank. I recognized the weapon in her hands. "The police," she went on, "do not yet know that the letter of introduction you brought to the captain was signed by a man who addressed Fraser-Freer as Dear Cousin, but who is completely unknown to the family. Once that information reaches Scotland Yard, your chance of escaping arrest is slim.

"They may not be able to fasten this crime upon you, but there will be complications most distasteful. One's liberty is well worth keeping—and then, too, before the case ends, there will be wide publicity—"

"Well?" said I.

"That is why you are going to suffer a lapse of memory in the matter of the hour at which you heard that struggle. As you think it over, it is going to occur to you that it may have been six-thirty, not seven. Otherwise—"

"Go on."

"Otherwise the letter of introduction you gave to the captain will be sent anonymously to Inspector Bray."

"You have that letter!" I cried.

"Not I," she answered. "But it will be sent to Bray. It will be pointed out to him that you were posing under false colors. You could not escape!"

I was most uncomfortable. The net of suspicion seemed closing in about me. But I was resentful, too, of the confidence in this woman's voice.

"None the less," said I, "I refuse to change my testimony. The truth is the truth—"

The woman had moved to the door. She turned.

"To-morrow," she replied, "it is not unlikely you will see Inspector Bray. As I said, I came here to give you advice. You had better take it. What does it matter—a half-hour this way or that? And the difference is prison for you. Good night."

She was gone. I followed into the hall. Below, in the street, I heard the rattle of her taxi.

I went back into my room and sat down. I was upset, and no mistake. Outside my windows the continuous symphony of the city played on—the busses, the trains, the never-silent voices. I gazed out. What a tremendous acreage of dank brick houses and dank British souls! I felt horribly alone. I may add that I felt a bit frightened, as though that great city were slowly closing in on me.

Who was this woman of mystery? What place had she held in the life—and perhaps in the death—of Captain Fraser-Freer? Why should she come boldly to my rooms to make her impossible demand?

I resolved that, even at the risk of my own comfort, I would stick to the truth. And to that resolve I would have clung had I not shortly received another visit—this one far more inexplicable, far more surprising, than the first.

It was about nine o'clock when Walters tapped at my door and told me two gentlemen wished to see me. A moment later into my study walked Lieutenant Norman Fraser-Freer and a fine old gentleman with a face that suggested some faded portrait hanging on an aristocrat's wall. I had never seen him before.

"I hope it is quite convenient for you to see us," said young Fraser-Freer.

I assured him that it was. The boy's face was drawn and haggard; there was terrible suffering in his eyes, yet about him hung, like a halo, the glory of a great resolution.

"May I present my father?" he said. "General Fraser-Freer, retired. We have come on a matter of supreme importance—"

The old man muttered something I could not catch. I could see that he had been hard hit by the loss of his elder son. I asked them to be seated; the general complied, but the boy walked the floor in a manner most distressing.

"I shall not be long," he remarked. "Nor at a time like this is one in the mood to be diplomatic. I will only say, sir, that we have come to ask of you a great—a very great favor indeed. You may not see fit to grant it. If that is the case we can not well reproach you. But if you can—"

"It is a great favor, sir!" broke in the general. "And I am in the odd position where I do not know whether you will serve me best by granting it or by refusing to do so."

"Father—please—if you don't mind—" The boy's voice was kindly but determined. He turned to me.

"Sir—you have testified to the police that it was a bit past seven when you heard in the room above the sounds of the struggle which—which—You understand."

In view of the mission of the caller who had departed a scant hour previously, the boy's question startled me.

"Such was my testimony," I answered. "It was the truth."

"Naturally," said Lieutenant Fraser-Freer. "But—er—as a matter of fact, we are here to ask that you alter your testimony. Could you, as a favor to us who have suffered so cruel a loss—a favor we should never forget—could you not make the hour of that struggle half after six?"

I was quite overwhelmed.

"Your—reasons?" I managed at last to ask.

"I am not able to give them to you in full," the boy answered. "I can only say this: It happens that at seven o'clock last Thursday night I was dining with friends at the Savoy—friends who would not be likely to forget the occasion."

The old general leaped to his feet.

"Norman," he cried, "I can not let you do this thing! I simply will not—"

"Hush, father," said the boy wearily. "We have threshed it all out. You have promised—"

The old man sank back into the chair and buried his face in his hands.

"If you are willing to change your testimony," young Fraser-Freer went on to me, "I shall at once confess to the police that it was I who—who murdered my brother. They suspect me. They know that late last Thursday afternoon I purchased a revolver, for which, they believe, at the last moment I substituted the knife. They know that I was in debt to him; that we had quarreled about money matters; that by his death I, and I alone, could profit."

He broke off suddenly and came toward me, holding out his arms with a pleading gesture I can never forget.

"Do this for me!" he cried. "Let me confess! Let me end this whole horrible business here and now."

Surely no man had ever to answer such an appeal before.

"Why?" I found myself saying, and over and over I repeated it: "Why? Why?"

The lieutenant faced me, and I hope never again to see such a look in a man's eyes.

"I loved him!" he cried. "That is why. For his honor, for the honor of our family, I am making this request of you. Believe me, it is not easy. I can tell you no more than that. You knew my brother?"

"Slightly."

"Then, for his sake—do this thing I ask."

"But—murder—"

"You heard the sounds of a struggle. I shall say that we quarreled—that I struck in self-defense." He turned to his father. "It will mean only a few years in prison—I can bear that!" he cried. "For the honor of our name!"

The old man groaned, but did not raise his head. The boy walked back and forth over my faded carpet like a lion caged. I stood wondering what answer I should make.

"I know what you are thinking," said the lieutenant. "You can not credit your ears. But you have heard correctly. And now—as you might put it—it is up to you. I have been in your country." He smiled pitifully. "I think I know you Americans. You are not the sort to refuse a man when he is sore beset—as I am."

I looked from him to the general and back again.

"I must think this over," I answered, my mind going at once to Colonel Hughes. "Later—say to-morrow—you shall have my decision."

"To-morrow," said the boy, "we shall both be called before Inspector Bray. I shall know your answer then—and I hope with all my heart it will be yes."

There were a few mumbled words of farewell and he and the broken old man went out. As soon as the street door closed behind them I hurried to the telephone and called a number Colonel Hughes had given me. It was with a feeling of relief that I heard his voice come back over the wire. I told him I must see him at once. He replied that by a singular chance he had been on the point of starting for my rooms.

In the half-hour that elapsed before the coming of the colonel I walked about like a man in a trance. He was barely inside my door when I began pouring out to him the story of those two remarkable visits. He made little comment on the woman's call beyond asking me whether I could describe her; and he smiled when I mentioned lilac perfume. At mention of young Fraser-Freer's preposterous request he whistled.

"By gad!" he said. "Interesting—most interesting! I am not surprised, however. That boy has the stuff in him."

"But what shall I do?" I demanded.

Colonel Hughes smiled.

"It makes little difference what you do," he said. "Norman Fraser-Freer did not kill his brother, and that will be proved in due time." He considered for a moment. "Bray no doubt would be glad to have you alter your testimony, since he is trying to fasten the crime on the young lieutenant. On the whole, if I were you, I think that when the opportunity comes to-morrow I should humor the inspector."

"You mean—tell him I am no longer certain as to the hour of that struggle?"

"Precisely. I give you my word that young Fraser-Freer will not be permanently incriminated by such an act on your part. And incidentally you will be aiding me."

"Very well," said I. "But I don't understand this at all."

"No—of course not. I wish I could explain to you; but I can not. I will say this—the death of Captain Fraser-Freer is regarded as a most significant thing by the War Office. Thus it happens that two distinct hunts for his assassin are under way— one conducted by Bray, the other by me. Bray does not suspect that I am working on the case and I want to keep him in the dark as long as possible. You may choose which of these investigations you wish to be identified with."

"I think," said I, "that I prefer you to Bray."

"Good boy!" he answered. "You have not gone wrong. And you can do me a service this evening, which is why I was on the point of coming here, even before you telephoned me. I take it that you remember and could identify the chap who called himself Archibald Enwright—the man who gave you that letter to the captain?"

"I surely could," said I.

"Then, if you can spare me an hour, get your hat."

And so it happens, lady of the Carlton, that I have just been to Limehouse. You do not know where Limehouse is and I trust you never will. It is picturesque; it is revolting; it is colorful and wicked. The weird odors of it still fill my nostrils; the sinister portrait of it is still before my eyes. It is the Chinatown of London—Limehouse. Down in the dregs of the town—with West India Dock Road for its spinal column—it lies, redolent of ways that are dark and tricks that are vain. Not only the heathen Chinee so peculiar shuffles through its dim-lit alleys, but the scum of the earth, of many colors and of many climes. The Arab and the Hindu, the Malayan and the Jap, black men from the Congo and fair men from Scandinavia—these you may meet there—the outpourings of all the ships that sail the Seven Seas. There many drunken beasts, with their pay in their pockets, seek each his favorite sin; and for those who love most the opium, there is, at all too regular intervals, the Sign of the Open Lamp.

We went there, Colonel Hughes and I. Up and down the narrow Causeway, yellow at intervals with the light from gloomy shops, dark mostly because of tightly closed shutters through which only thin jets found their way, we walked until we came and stood at last in shadow outside the black doorway of Harry San Li's so-called restaurant. We waited ten, fifteen minutes; then a man came down the Causeway and paused before that door. There was something familiar in his jaunty walk. Then the faint glow of the lamp that was the indication of Harry San's real business lit his pale face, and I knew that I had seen him last in the cool evening at Interlaken, where Limehouse could not have lived a moment, with the Jungfrau frowning down upon it.

"Enwright?" whispered Hughes.

"Not a doubt of it!" said I.

"Good!" he replied with fervor.

And now another man shuffled down the street and stood suddenly straight and waiting before the colonel.

"Stay with him," said Hughes softly. "Don't let him get out of your sight."

"Very good, sir," said the man; and, saluting, he passed on up the stairs and whistled softly at that black depressing door.

The clock above the Millwall Docks was striking eleven as the colonel and I caught a bus that should carry us back to a brighter, happier London. Hughes spoke but seldom on that ride; and, repeating his advice that I humor Inspector Bray on the morrow, he left me in the Strand.

So, my lady, here I sit in my study, waiting for that most important day that is shortly to dawn. A full evening, you must admit. A woman with the perfume of lilacs about her has threatened that unless I lie I shall encounter consequences most unpleasant. A handsome young lieutenant has begged me to tell that same lie for the honor of his family, and thus condemn him to certain arrest and imprisonment. And I have been down into hell, to-night and seen Archibald Enwright, of Interlaken, conniving with the devil.

I presume I should go to bed; but I know I can not sleep. To-morrow is to be, beyond all question, a red-letter day in the matter of the captain's murder. And once again, against my will, I am down to play a leading part.

The symphony of this great, gray, sad city is a mere hum in the distance now, for it is nearly midnight. I shall mail this letter to you—post it, I should say, since I am in London—and then I shall wait in my dim rooms for the dawn. And as I wait I shall be thinking not always of the captain, or his brother, or Hughes, or Limehouse and Enwright, but often—oh, very often—of you.

In my last letter I scoffed at the idea of a great war. But when we came back from Limehouse to-night the papers told us that the Kaiser had signed the order to mobilize. Austria in; Serbia in; Germany, Russia and France in. Hughes tells me that England is shortly to follow, and I suppose there is no doubt of it. It is a frightful thing—this future that looms before us; and I pray that for you at least it may hold only happiness.

For, my lady, when I write good night, I speak it aloud as I write; and there is in my voice more than I dare tell you of now.

THE AGONY COLUMN MAN.

Not unwelcome to the violet eyes of the girl from Texas were the last words of this letter, read in her room that Sunday morning. But the lines predicting England's early entrance into the war recalled to her mind a most undesirable contingency. On the previous night, when the war extras came out confirming the forecast of his favorite bootblack, her usually calm father had shown signs of panic. He was not a man slow to act. And she knew that, putty though he was in her hands in matters which he did not regard as important, he could also be firm where he thought firmness necessary. America looked even better to him than usual, and he had made up his mind to go there immediately. There was no use in arguing with him.

At this point came a knock at her door and her father entered. One look at his face—red, perspiring and decidedly unhappy—served to cheer his daughter.

"Been down to the steamship offices," he panted, mopping his bald head. "They're open today, just like it was a week day—but they might as well be closed. There's nothing doing. Every boat's booked up to the rails; we can't get out of here for two weeks—maybe more."

"I'm sorry," said his daughter.

"No, you ain't! You're delighted! You think it's romantic to get caught like this. Wish I had the enthusiasm of youth." He fanned himself with a newspaper. "Lucky I went over to the express office yesterday and loaded up on gold. I reckon when the blow falls it'll be tolerable hard to cash checks in this man's town."

"That was a good idea."

"Ready for breakfast?" he inquired.

"Quite ready," she smiled.

They went below, she humming a song from a revue, while he glared at her. She was very glad they were to be in London a little longer. She felt she could not go, with that mystery still unsolved.

CHAPTER SIX

The last peace Sunday London was to know in many weary months went by, a tense and anxious day. Early on Monday the fifth letter from the young man of the Agony Column arrived, and when the girl from Texas read it she knew that under no circumstances could she leave London now.

It ran:

DEAR LADY FROM HOME: I call you that because the word home has for me, this hot afternoon in London, about the sweetest sound word ever had. I can see, when I close my eyes, Broadway at midday; Fifth Avenue, gay and colorful, even with all the best people away; Washington Square, cool under the trees, lovely and desirable despite the presence everywhere of alien neighbors from the district to the South. I long for home with an ardent longing; never was London so cruel, so hopeless, so drab, in my eyes. For, as I write this, a constable sits at my elbow, and he and I are shortly to start for Scotland Yard. I have been arrested as a suspect in the case of Captain Fraser-Freer's murder!

I predicted last night that this was to be a red-letter day in the history of that case, and I also saw myself an unwilling actor in the drama. But little did I suspect the series of astonishing events that was to come with the morning; little did I dream that the net I have been dreading would today engulf me. I can scarcely blame Inspector Bray for holding me; what I can not understand is why Colonel Hughes—

But you want, of course, the whole story from the beginning; and I shall give it to you. At eleven o'clock this morning a constable called on me at my rooms and informed me that I was wanted at once by the Chief Inspector at the Yard.

We climbed—the constable and I—a narrow stone stairway somewhere at the back of New Scotland Yard, and so came to the inspector's room. Bray was waiting for us, smiling and confident. I remember—silly as the detail is—that he wore in his buttonhole a white rose. His manner of greeting me was more genial than usual. He began by informing me that the police had apprehended the man who, they believed, was guilty of the captain's murder.

"There is one detail to be cleared up," he said. "You told me the other night that it was shortly after seven o'clock when you heard the sounds of struggle in the room above you. You were somewhat excited at the time, and under similar circumstances men have been known to make mistakes. Have you considered the matter since? Is it not possible that you were in error in regard to the hour?"

I recalled Hughes' advice to humor the inspector; and I said that, having thought it over, I was not quite sure. It might have been earlier than seven—say six-thirty.

"Exactly," said Bray. He seemed rather pleased. "The natural stress of the moment—I understand. Wilkinson, bring in your prisoner. The constable addressed turned and left the room, coming back a moment later with Lieutenant Norman Fraser-Freer. The boy was pale; I could see at a glance that he had not slept for several nights.

"Lieutenant," said Bray very sharply, "will you tell me—is it true that your brother, the late captain, had loaned you a large sum of money a year or so ago?"

"Quite true," answered the lieutenant in a low voice.

"You and he had quarreled about the amount of money you spent?"

"Yes."

"By his death you became the sole heir of your father, the general. Your position with the money-lenders was quite altered. Am I right?"

"I fancy so."

"Last Thursday afternoon you went to the Army and Navy Stores and purchased a revolver. You already had your service weapon, but to shoot a man with a bullet from that would be to make the hunt of the police for the murderer absurdly simple."

The boy made no answer.

"Let us suppose," Bray went on, "that last Thursday evening at half after six you called on your brother in his rooms at Adelphi Terrace. There was an argument about money. You became enraged. You saw him and him alone between you and the fortune you needed so badly. Then—I am only supposing—you noticed on his table an odd knife he had brought from India—safer—more silent—than a gun. You seized it—"

"Why suppose?" the boy broke in. "I'm not trying to conceal anything. You're right—I did it! I killed my brother! Now let us get the whole business over as soon as may be."

Into the face of Inspector Bray there came at that moment a look that has puzzling me ever since—a look that has recurred to my mind again and again,—in the stress and storm of this eventful day. It was only too evident that this confession came to him as a shock. I presume so easy a victory seemed hollow to him; he was wishing the boy had put up a fight. Policemen are probably like that.

"My boy," he said, "I am sorry for you. My course is clear. If you will go with one of my men—"

It was at this point that the door of the inspector's room opened and Colonel Hughes, cool and smiling, walked in. Bray chuckled at sight of the military man.

"Ah, Colonel," he cried, "you make a good entrance! This morning, when I discovered that I had the honor of having you associated with me in the search for the captain's murderer, you were foolish enough to make a little wager—"

"I remember," Hughes answered. "A scarab pin against—a Homburg hat."

"Precisely," said Bray. "You wagered that you, and not I, would discover the guilty man. Well, Colonel, you owe me a scarab. Lieutenant Norman Fraser-Freer has just told me that he killed his brother, and I was on the point of taking down his full confession."

"Indeed!" replied Hughes calmly. "Interesting—most interesting! But before we consider the wager lost—before you force the lieutenant to confess in full—I should like the floor."

"Certainly," smiled Bray.

"When you were kind enough to let me have two of your men this morning," said Hughes, "I told you I contemplated the arrest of a lady. I have brought that lady to Scotland Yard with me." He stepped to the door, opened it and beckoned. A tall, blonde handsome woman of about thirty-five entered; and instantly to my nostrils came the pronounced odor of lilacs. "Allow me, Inspector," went on the colonel, "to introduce to you the Countess Sophie de Graf, late of Berlin, late of Delhi and Rangoon, now of 17 Leitrim Grove, Battersea Park Road."

The woman faced Bray; and there was a terrified, hunted look in her eyes.

"You are the inspector?" she asked.

"I am," said Bray.

"And a man—I can see that," she went on, her flashing angrily at Hughes. "I appeal to you to protect me from the brutal questioning of this—this fiend."

"You are hardly complimentary, Countess," Hughes smiled. "But I am willing to forgive you if you will tell the inspector the story that you have recently related to me."

The woman shut her lips tightly and for a long moment gazed into the eyes of Inspector Bray.

"He—" She said at last, nodding in the direction of Colonel Hughes, "—he got it out of me—how, I don't know."

"Got what out of you?" Bray's little eyes were blinking.

"At six-thirty o'clock last Thursday evening," said the woman, "I went to the rooms of Captain Fraser-Freer, in Adelphi Terrace. An argument arose. I seized from his table an Indian dagger that was lying there—I stabbed him just above the heart!"

In that room in Scotland Yard a tense silence fell. For the first time we were all conscious of a tiny clock on the inspector's desk, for it ticked now with a loudness sudden and startling. I gazed at the faces about me. Bray's showed a momentary surprise—then the mask fell again. Lieutenant Fraser-Freer was plainly amazed. On the face of Colonel Hughes I saw what struck me as an open sneer.

"Go on, Countess," he smiled.

She shrugged her shoulders and turned toward him a disdainful back. Her eyes were all for Bray.

"It's very brief, the story," she said hastily—I thought almost apologetically. "I had known the captain in Rangoon. My husband was in business there—an exporter of rice—and Captain Fraser-Freer came often to our house. We—he was a charming man, the captain—"

"Go on!" ordered Hughes.

"We fell desperately in love," said the countess. "When he returned to England, though supposedly on a furlough, he told me he would never return to Rangoon. He expected a transfer to Egypt. So it was arranged that I should desert my husband and follow on the next boat. I did so—believing in the captain—thinking he really cared for me—I gave up everything for him. And then—"

Her voice broke and she took out a handkerchief. Again that odor of lilacs in the room.

"For a time I saw the captain often in London; and then I began to notice a change. Back among his own kind, with the lonely days in India a mere memory—he seemed no longer to—to care for me. Then—last Thursday morning—he called on me to tell me that he was through; that he would never see me again—in fact, that he was to marry a girl of his own people who had been waiting—"

The woman looked piteously about at us.

"I was desperate," she pleaded. "I had given up all that life held for me—given it up for a man who now looked at me coldly and spoke of marrying another. Can you wonder that I went in the evening to his rooms—went to plead with him—to beg, almost on my knees? It was no use. He was done with me—he said that over and over. Overwhelmed with blind rage and despair, I snatched up that knife from the table and plunged it into his heart. At once I was filled with remorse. I—"

"One moment," broke in Hughes. "You may keep the details of your subsequent actions until later. I should like to compliment you, Countess. You tell it better each time."

He came over and faced Bray. I thought there was a distinct note of hostility in his voice.

"Checkmate, Inspector!" he said. Bray made no reply. He sat there staring up at the colonel, his face turned to stone.

"The scarab pin," went on Hughes, "is not yet forthcoming. We are tied for honors, my friend. You have your confession, but I have one to match it."

"All this is beyond me," snapped Bray.

"A bit beyond me, too," the colonel answered. "Here are two people who wish us to believe that on the evening of Thursday last, at half after six of the clock, each sought out Captain Fraser-Freer in his rooms and murdered him."

He walked to the window and then wheeled dramatically.

"The strangest part of it all is," he added, "that at six-thirty o'clock last Thursday evening, at an obscure restaurant in Soho—Frigacci's—these two people were having tea together!"

I must admit that, as the colonel calmly offered this information, I suddenly went limp all over at a realization of the endless maze of mystery in which we were involved. The woman gave a little cry and Lieutenant Fraser-Freer leaped to his feet.

"How the devil do you know that?" he cried.

"I know it," said Colonel Hughes, "because one of my men happened to be having tea at a table near by. He happened to be having tea there for the reason that ever since the arrival of this lady in London, at the request of—er—friends in India, I have been keeping track of her every move; just as I kept watch over your late brother, the captain."

Without a word Lieutenant Fraser-Freer dropped into a chair and buried his face in his hands.

"I'm sorry, my son," said Hughes. "Really, I am. You made a heroic effort to keep the facts from coming out—a man's-size effort it was. But the War Office knew long before you did that your brother had succumbed to this woman's lure—that he was serving her and Berlin, and not his own country, England."

Fraser-Freer raised his head. When he spoke there was in his voice an emotion vastly more sincere than that which had. moved him when he made his absurd confession.

"The game's up," he said. "I have done all I could. This will kill my father, I am afraid. Ours has been an honorable name, Colonel; you know that—a long line of military men whose loyalty to their country has never before been in question. I thought my confession would and the whole nasty business, that the investigations would stop, and that I might be able to keep forever unknown this horrible thing about him—about my brother."

Colonel Hughes laid his hand on the boy's shoulder, and the latter went on: "They reached me—those frightful insinuations about Stephen—in a round about way; and when he came home from India I resolved to watch him. I saw him go often to the house of this woman. I satisfied myself that she was the same one involved in the stories coming from Rangoon; then, under another name, I managed to meet her. I hinted to her that I myself was none too loyal; not completely, but to a limited extent, I won her confidence. Gradually I became convinced that my brother was indeed disloyal to his country, to his name, to us all. It was at that tea time you have mentioned when I finally made up my mind. I had already bought a revolver; and, with it in my pocket, I went to the Savoy for dinner."

He rose and paced the floor.

"I left the Savoy early and went to Stephen's rooms. I was resolved to have it out with him, to put the matter to him bluntly; and if he had no explanation to give me I intended to kill him then and there. So, you see, I was guilty in intention if not in reality. I entered his study. It was filled with strangers. On his sofa I saw my brother Stephen lying—stabbed above the heart—dead!" There was a moment's silence. "That is all," said Lieutenant Fraser-Freer.

"I take it," said Hughes kindly, "that we have finished with the lieutenant. Eh, Inspector?"

"Yes," said Bray shortly. "You may go."

"Thank you," the boy answered. As he went out he said brokenly to Hughes: "I must find him—my father."

Bray sat in his chair, staring hard ahead, his jaw thrust out angrily. Suddenly he turned on Hughes.

"You don't play fair," he said. "I wasn't told anything of the status of the captain at the War Office. This is all news to me."

"Very well," smiled Hughes. "The bet is off if you like."

"No, by heaven!" Bray cried. "It's still on, and I'll win it yet. A fine morning's work I suppose you think you've done. But are we any nearer to finding the murderer? Tell me that."

"Only a bit nearer, at any rate," replied Hughes suavely. "This lady, of course, remains in custody."

"Yes, yes," answered the inspector. "Take her away!" he ordered.

A constable came forward for the countess and Colonel Hughes gallantly held open the door.

"You will have an opportunity, Sophie," he said, "to think up another story. You are clever—it will not be hard."

She gave him a black look and went out. Bray got up from his desk. He and Colonel Hughes stood facing each other across a table, and to me there was something in the manner of each that suggested eternal conflict.

"Well?" sneered Bray.

"There is one possibility we have overlooked," Hughes answered. He turned toward me and I was startled by the coldness in his eyes. "Do you know, Inspector," he went on, "that this American came to London with a letter of introduction to the captain—a letter from the captain's cousin, one Archibald Enwright? And do you know that Fraser-Freer had no cousin of that name?"

"No!" said Bray.

"It happens to be the truth," said Hughes. "The American has confessed as much to me."

"Then," said Bray to me, and his little blinking eyes were on me with a narrow calculating glance that sent the shivers up and down my spine, "you are under arrest. I have exempted you so far because of your friend at the United States Consulate. That exemption ends now."

I was thunderstruck. I turned to the colonel, the man who had suggested that I seek him out if I needed a friend—the man I had looked to to save me from just such a contingency as this. But his eyes were quite fishy and unsympathetic.

"Quite correct, Inspector," he said. "Lock him up!" And as I began to protest he passed very close to me and spoke in a low voice: "Say nothing. Wait!"

I pleaded to be allowed to go back to my rooms, to communicate with my friends, and pay a visit to our consulate and to the Embassy; and at the colonel's suggestion Bray agreed to this somewhat irregular course. So this afternoon I have been abroad with a constable, and while I wrote this long letter to you he has been fidgeting in my easy chair. Now he informs me that his patience is exhausted and that I must go at once. So there is no time to wonder; no time to speculate as to the future, as to the colonel's sudden turn against me or the promise of his whisper in my ear. I shall, no doubt, spend the night behind those hideous, forbidding walls that your guide has pointed out to you as New Scotland Yard. And when I shall write again, when I shall end this series of letters so filled with—

The constable will not wait. He is as impatient as a child. Surely he is lying when he says I have kept him here an hour.

Wherever I am, dear lady, whatever be the end of this amazing tangle, you may be sure the thought of you—Confound the man!

YOURS, IN DURANCE VILE.

This fifth letter from the young man of the Agony Column arrived at the Carlton Hotel, as the reader may recall, on Monday morning, August the third. And it represented to the girl from Texas the climax of the excitement she had experienced in the matter of the murder in Adelphi Terrace. The news that her pleasant young friend—whom she did not know—had been arrested as a suspect in the case, inevitable as it had seemed for days, came none the less as an unhappy shock. She wondered whether there was anything she could do to help. She even considered going to Scotland Yard and, on the ground that her father was a Congressman from Texas, demanding the immediate release of her strawberry man. Sensibly, however, she decided that Congressmen from Texas meant little in the life of the London police. Besides, she night have difficulty in explaining to that same Congressman how she happened to know all about a crime that was as yet unmentioned in the newspapers.

So she reread the latter portion of the fifth letter, which pictured her hero marched off ingloriously to Scotland Yard and with a worried little sigh, went below to join her father.

CHAPTER SEVEN

In the course of the morning she made several mysterious inquiries of her parent regarding nice points of international law as it concerned murder, and it is probable that he would have been struck by the odd nature of these questions had he not been unduly excited about another matter.

"I tell you, we've got to get home!" he announced gloomily. "The German troops are ready at Aix-la-Chapelle for an assault on Liege. Yes, sir—they're going to strike through Belgium! Know what that means? England in the war! Labor troubles; suffragette troubles; civil war in Ireland—these things will melt away as quickly as that snow we had last winter in Texas. They'll go in. It would be national suicide if they didn't."

His daughter stared at him. She was unaware that it was the bootblack at the Carlton he was now quoting. She began to think he knew more about foreign affairs than she had given him credit for.

"Yes, sir," he went on; "we've got to travel—fast. This won't be a healthy neighborhood for non-combatants when the ruction starts. I'm going if I have to buy a liner!"

"Nonsense!" said the girl. "This is the chance of a lifetime. I won't be cheated out of it by a silly old dad. Why, here we are, face to face with history!"

"American history is good enough for me," he spread-eagled. "What are you looking at?"

"Provincial to the death!" she said thoughtfully. "You old dear—I love you so! Some of our statesmen over home are going to look pretty foolish now in the face of things they can't understand, I hope you're not going to be one of them."

"Twaddle!" he cried. "I'm going to the steamship offices today and argue as I never argued for a vote."

His daughter saw that he was determined; and, wise from long experience, she did not try to dissuade him.

London that hot Monday was a city on the alert, a city of hearts heavy with dread. The rumors in one special edition of the papers were denied in the next and reaffirmed in the next. Men who could look into the future walked the streets with faces far from happy. Unrest ruled the town. And it found its echo in the heart of the girl from Texas as she thought of her young friend of the Agony Column "in durance vile" behind the frowning walls of Scotland Yard.

That afternoon her father appeared, with the beaming mien of the victor, and announced that for a stupendous sum he had bought the tickets of a man who was to have sailed on the steamship Saronia three days hence.

"The boat train leaves at ten Thursday morning," he said. "Take your last look at Europe and be ready."

Three days! His daughter listened with sinking heart. Could she in three days' time learn the end of that strange mystery, know the final fate of the man who had first addressed her so unconventionally in a public print? Why, at the end of three days he might still be in Scotland Yard, a prisoner! She could not leave if that were true—she simply could not. Almost she was on the point of telling her father the story of the whole affair, confident that she could soothe his anger and enlist his aid. She decided to wait until the next morning; and, if no letter came then—

But on Tuesday morning a letter did come and the beginning of it brought pleasant news. The beginning—yes. But the end! This was the letter:

DEAR ANXIOUS LADY: Is it too much for me to assume that you have been just that, knowing as you did that I was locked up for the murder of a captain in the Indian Army, with the evidence all against me and hope a very still small voice indeed?

Well, dear lady, be anxious no longer. I have just lived through the most astounding day of all the astounding days that have been my portion since last Thursday. And now, in the dusk, I sit again in my rooms, a free man, and write to you in what peace and quiet I can command after the startling adventure through which I have recently passed.

Suspicion no longer points to me; constables no longer eye me; Scotland Yard is not even slightly interested in me. For the murderer of Captain Fraser-Freer has been caught at last!

Sunday night I spent ingloriously in a cell in Scotland Yard. I could not sleep. I had so much to think of—you, for example, and at intervals how I might escape from the folds of the net that had closed so tightly about me. My friend at the consulate, Watson, called on me late in the evening; and he was very kind. But there was a note lacking in his voice, and after he was gone the terrible certainty came into my mind—he believed that I was guilty after all.

The night passed, and a goodly portion of today went by—as the poets say—with lagging feet. I thought of London, yellow in the sun. I thought of the Carlton—I suppose there are no more strawberries by this time. And my waiter—that stiff-backed Prussian—is home in Deutschland now, I presume, marching with his regiment. I thought of you.

At three o'clock this afternoon they came for me and I was led back to the room belonging to Inspector Bray. When I entered, however, the inspector was not there—only Colonel Hughes, immaculate and self-possessed, as usual, gazing out the window into the cheerless stone court. He turned when I entered. I suppose I must have had a most woebegone appearance, for a look of regret crossed his face.

"My dear fellow," he cried, "my most humble apologies! I intended to have you released last night. But, believe me, I have been frightfully busy."

I said nothing. What could I say? The fact that he had been busy struck me as an extremely silly excuse. But the inference that my escape from the toils of the law was imminent set my heart to thumping.

"I fear you can never forgive me for throwing you over as I did yesterday," he went on. "I can only say that it was absolutely necessary—as you shall shortly understand."

I thawed a bit. After all, there was an unmistakable sincerity in his voice and manner.

"We are waiting for Inspector Bray," continued the colonel. "I take it you wish to see this thing through?"

"To the end," I answered.

"Naturally. The inspector was called away yesterday immediately after our interview with him. He had business on the Continent, I understand. But fortunately I managed to reach him at Dover and he has come back to London. I wanted him, you see, because I have found the murderer of Captain Fraser-Freer."

I thrilled to hear that, for from my point of view it was certainly a consummation devoutly to be wished. The colonel did not speak again. In a few minutes the door opened and Bray came in. His clothes looked as though he had slept in them; his little eyes were bloodshot. But in those eyes there was a fire I shall never forget. Hughes bowed.

"Good afternoon, Inspector," he said. "I'm really sorry I had to interrupt you as I did; but I most awfully wanted you to know that you owe me a Homburg hat." He went closer to the detective. "You see, I have won that wager. I have found the man who murdered Captain Fraser-Freer."

Curiously enough, Bray said nothing. He sat down at his desk and idly glanced through the pile of mail that lay upon it. Finally he looked up and said in a weary tone:

"You're very clever, I'm sure, Colonel Hughes."

"Oh—I wouldn't say that," replied Hughes. "Luck was with me—from the first. I am really very glad to have been of service in the matter, for I am convinced that if I had not taken part in the search it would have gone hard with some innocent man."

Bray's big pudgy hands still played idly with the mail on his desk. Hughes went on: "Perhaps, as a clever detective, you will be interested in the series of events which enabled me to win that Homburg hat? You have heard, no doubt, that the man I have caught is Von der Herts—ten years ago the best secret-service man in the employ of the Berlin government, but for the past few years mysteriously missing from our line of vision. We've been wondering about him—at the War Office."

The colonel dropped into a chair, facing Bray.

"You know Von der Herts, of course?" he remarked casually.

"Of course," said Bray, still in that dead tired voice.

"He is the head of that crowd in England," went on Hughes. "Rather a feather in my cap to get him—but I mustn't boast. Poor Fraser-Freer would have got him if I hadn't—only Von der Herts had the luck to get the captain first."

Bray raised his eyes.

"You said you were going to tell me—" he began.

"And so I am," said Hughes. "Captain Fraser-Freer got in rather a mess in India and failed of promotion. It was suspected that he was discontented, soured on the Service; and the Countess Sophie de Graf was set to beguile him with her charms, to kill his loyalty and win him over to her crowd.

"It was thought she had succeeded—the Wilhelmstrasse thought so—we at the War Office thought so, as long as he stayed in India.

"But when the captain and the woman came on to London we discovered that we had done him a great injustice. He let us know, when the first chance offered, that he was trying to redeem himself, to round up a dangerous band of spies by pretending to be one of them. He said that it was his mission in London to meet Von der Herts, the greatest of them all; and that, once he had located this man, we would hear from him again. In the weeks that followed I continued to keep a watch on the countess; and I kept track of the captain, too, in a general way, for I'm ashamed to say I was not quite sure of him."

The colonel got up and walked to the window; then turned and continued: "Captain Fraser-Freer and Von der Herts were completely unknown to each other. The mails were barred as a means of communication; but Fraser-Freer knew that in some way word from the master would reach him, and he had had a tip to watch the personal column of the Daily Mail. Now we have the explanation of those four odd messages. From that column the man from Rangoon learned that he was to wear a white aster in his button-hole, a scarab pin in his tie, a Homburg hat on his head, and meet Von der Herts at Ye Old Gambrinus Restaurant in Regent Street, last Thursday night at ten o'clock. As we know, he made all arrangements to comply with those directions. He made other arrangements as well. Since it was out of the question for him to come to Scotland Yard, by skillful maneuvering he managed to interview an inspector of police at the Hotel Cecil. It was agreed that on Thursday night Von der Herts would be placed under arrest the moment he made himself known to the captain."

Hughes paused. Bray still idled with his pile of letters, while the colonel regarded him gravely.

"Poor Fraser-Freer!" Hughes went on. "Unfortunately for him, Von der Herts knew almost as soon as did the inspector that a plan was afoot to trap him. There was but one course open to him: He located the captain's lodgings, went there at seven that night, and killed a loyal and brave Englishman where he stood."

A tense silence filled the room. I sat on the edge of my chair, wondering just where all this unwinding of the tangle was leading us.

"I had little, indeed, to work on," went on Hughes. "But I had this advantage: the spy thought the police, and the police alone, were seeking the murderer. He was at no pains to throw me off his track, because he did not suspect that I was on it. For weeks my men had been watching the countess. I had them continue to do so. I figured that sooner or later Von der Herts would get in touch with her. I was right. And when at last I saw with my own eyes the man who must, beyond all question, be Von der Herts, I was astounded, my dear Inspector, I was overwhelmed."

"Yes?" said Bray.

"I set to work then in earnest to connect him with that night in Adelphi Terrace. All the finger marks in the captain's study were for some reason destroyed, but I found others outside, in the dust on that seldom-used gate which leads from the garden. Without his knowing, I secured from the man I suspected the imprint of his right thumb. A comparison was startling. Next I went down into Fleet Street and luckily managed to get hold of the typewritten copy sent to the Mail bearing those four messages. I noticed that in these the letter a was out of alignment. I maneuvered to get a letter written on a typewriter belonging to my man. The a was out of alignment. Then Archibald Enwright, a renegade and waster well known to us as serving other countries, came to England. My man and he met—at Ye Old Gambrinus, in Regent Street. And finally, on a visit to the lodgings of this man who, I was now certain, was Von der Herts, under the mattress of his bed I found this knife."

And Colonel Hughes threw down upon the inspector's desk the knife from India that I had last seen in the study of Captain Fraser-Freer.

"All these points of evidence were in my hands yesterday morning in this room," Hughes went on. "Still, the answer they gave me was so unbelievable, so astounding, I was not satisfied; I wanted even stronger proof. That is why I directed suspicion to my American friend here. I was waiting. I knew that at last Von der Herts realized the danger he was in. I felt that if opportunity were offered he would attempt to escape from England; and then our proofs of his guilt would be unanswerable, despite his cleverness. True enough, in the afternoon he secured the release of the countess, and together they started for the Continent. I was lucky enough to get him at Dover—and glad to let the lady go on."

And now, for the first time, the startling truth struck me full in the face as Hughes smiled down at his victim.

"Inspector Bray," he said, "or Von der Herts, as you choose, I arrest you on two counts: First, as the head of the Wilhelmstrasse spy system in England; second, as the murderer of Captain Fraser-Freer. And, if you will allow me, I wish to compliment you on your efficiency."

Bray did not reply for a moment. I sat numb in my chair. Finally the inspector looked up. He actually tried to smile.

"You win the hat," he said, "but you must go to Homburg for it. I will gladly pay all expenses."

"Thank you," answered Hughes. "I hope to visit your country before long; but I shall not be occupied with hats. Again I congratulate you. You were a bit careless, but your position justified that. As head of the department at Scotland Yard given over to the hunt for spies, precaution doubtless struck you as unnecessary. How unlucky for poor Fraser-Freer that it was to you he went to arrange for your own arrest! I got that information from a clerk at the Cecil. You were quite right, from your point of view, to kill him. And, as I say, you could afford to be rather reckless. You had arranged that when the news of his murder came to Scotland Yard you yourself would be on hand to conduct the search for the guilty man. A happy situation, was it not?"

"It seemed so at the time," admitted Bray; and at last I thought I detected a note of bitterness in his voice.

"I'm very sorry—really," said Hughes. "Today, or tomorrow at the latest, England will enter the war. You know what that means, Von der Herts. The Tower of London—and a firing squad!"

Deliberately he walked away from the inspector, and stood facing the window. Von der Herts was fingering idly that Indian knife which lay on his desk. With a quick hunted look about the room, he raised his hand; and before I could leap forward to stop him he had plunged the knife into his heart.

Colonel Hughes turned round at my cry, but even at what met his eyes now that Englishman was imperturbable.

"Too bad!" he said. "Really too bad! The man had courage and, beyond all doubt, brains. But—this is most considerate of him. He has saved me such a lot of trouble."

The colonel effected my release at once; and he and I walked down Whitehall together in the bright sun that seemed so good to me after the bleak walls of the Yard. Again he apologized for turning suspicion my way the previous day; but I assured him I held no grudge for that.

"One or two things I do not understand," I said. "That letter I brought from Interlaken—"

"Simple enough," he replied. "Enwright—who, by the way, is now in the Tower—wanted to communicate with Fraser-Freer, who he supposed was a loyal member of the band. Letters sent by post seemed dangerous. With your kind assistance he informed the captain of his whereabouts and the date of his imminent arrival in London. Fraser-Freer, not wanting you entangled in his plans, eliminated you by denying the existence of this cousin—the truth, of course."

"Why," I asked, "did the countess call on me to demand that I alter my testimony?"

"Bray sent her. He had rifled Fraser-Freer's desk and he held that letter from Enwright. He was most anxious to fix the guilt upon the young lieutenant's head. You and your testimony as to the hour of the crime stood in the way. He sought to intimidate you with threats—"

"But—"

"I know—you are wondering why the countess confessed to me next day. I had the woman in rather a funk. In the meshes of my rapid-fire questioning she became hopelessly involved. This was because she was suddenly terrified she realized I must have been watching her for weeks, and that perhaps Von der Herts was not so immune from suspicion as he supposed. At the proper moment I suggested that I might have to take her to Inspector Bray. This gave her an idea. She made her fake confession to reach his side; once there, she warned him of his danger and they fled together."

We walked along a moment in silence. All about us the lurid special editions of the afternoon were flaunting their predictions of the horror to come. The face of the colonel was grave.

"How long had Von der Herts held his position at the Yard?" I asked.

"For nearly five years," Hughes answered.

"It seems incredible," I murmured.

"So it does," he answered; "but it is only the first of many incredible things that this war will reveal. Two months from now we shall all have forgotten it in the face of new revelations far more unbelievable." He sighed. "If these men about us realized the terrible ordeal that lies ahead! Misgoverned; unprepared—I shudder at the thought of the sacrifices we must make, many of them in vain. But I suppose that somehow, some day, we shall muddle through."

He bade me good-by in Trafalgar Square, saying that he must at once seek out the father and brother of the late captain, and tell them the news—that their kinsman was really loyal to his country.

"It will come to them as a ray of light in the dark—my news," he said. "And now, thank you once again."

We parted and I came back here to my lodgings. The mystery is finally solved, though in such a way it is difficult to believe that it was anything but a nightmare at any time. But solved none the less; and I should be at peace, except for one great black fact that haunts me, will not let me rest. I must tell you, dear lady—And yet I fear it means the end of everything. If only I can make you understand!

I have walked my floor, deep in thought, in puzzlement, in indecision. Now I have made up my mind. There is no other way—I must tell you the truth.

Despite the fact that Bray was Von der Herts; despite the fact that he killed himself at the discovery—despite this and that, and everything—Bray did not kill Captain Fraser-Freer!

On last Thursday evening, at a little after seven o'clock, I myself climbed the stairs, entered the captain's rooms, picked up that knife from his desk, and stabbed him just above the heart!

What provocation I was under, what stern necessity moved me—all this you must wait until to-morrow to know. I shall spend another anxious day preparing my defense, hoping that through some miracle of mercy you may forgive me— understand that there was nothing else I could do.

Do not judge, dear lady, until you know everything—until all my evidence is in your lovely hands.

YOURS, IN ALL HUMILITY.

The first few paragraphs of this the sixth and next to the last letter from the Agony Column man had brought a smile of relief to the face of the girl who read. She was decidedly glad to learn that her friend no longer languished back of those gray walls on Victoria Embankment. With excitement that increased as she went along, she followed Colonel Hughes as—in the letter—he moved nearer and nearer his denouement, until finally his finger pointed to Inspector Bray sitting guilty in his chair. This was an eminently satisfactory solution, and it served the inspector right for locking up her friend. Then, with the suddenness of a bomb from a Zeppelin, came, at the end, her strawberry man's confession of guilt. He was the murderer, after all! He admitted it! She could scarcely believe her eyes.

Yet there it was, in ink as violet as those eyes, on the note paper that had become so familiar to her during the thrilling week just past. She read it a second time, and yet a third. Her amazement gave way to anger; her cheeks flamed. Still—he had asked her not to judge until all his evidence was in. This was a reasonable request surely, and she could not in fairness refuse to grant it.

CHAPTER EIGHT

So began an anxious day, not only for the girl from Texas but for all London as well. Her father was bursting with new diplomatic secrets recently extracted from his bootblack adviser. Later, in Washington, he was destined to be a marked man because of his grasp of the situation abroad. No one suspected the bootblack, the power behind the throne; but the gentleman from Texas was destined to think of that able diplomat many times, and to wish that he still had him at his feet to advise him.

"War by midnight, sure!" he proclaimed on the morning of this fateful Tuesday. "I tell you, Marian, we're lucky to have our tickets on the Saronia. Five thousand dollars wouldn't buy them from me today! I'll be a happy man when we go aboard that liner day after to-morrow."

Day after to-morrow! The girl wondered. At any rate, she would have that last letter then—the letter that was to contain whatever defense her young friend could offer to explain his dastardly act. She waited eagerly for that final epistle.

The day dragged on, bringing at its close England's entrance into the war; and the Carlton bootblack was a prophet not without honor in a certain Texas heart. And on the following morning there arrived a letter which was torn open by eager trembling fingers. The letter spoke:

DEAR LADY JUDGE: This is by far the hardest to write of all the letters you have had from me. For twenty-four hours I have been planning it. Last night I walked on the Embankment while the hansoms jogged by and the lights of the tramcars danced on Westminster Bridge just as the fireflies used to in the garden back of our house in Kansas. While I walked I planned. Today, shut up in my rooms, I was also planning. And yet now, when I sit down to write, I am still confused; still at a loss where to begin and what to say, once I have begun.

At the close of my last letter I confessed to you that it was I who murdered Captain Fraser-Freer. That is the truth. Soften the blow as I may, it all comes down to that. The bitter truth!

Not a week ago—last Thursday night at seven—I climbed our dark stairs and plunged a knife into the heart of that defenseless gentleman. If only I could point out to you that he had offended me in some way; if I could prove to you that his death was necessary to me, as it really was to Inspector Bray—then there might be some hope of your ultimate pardon. But, alas! he had been most kind to me—kinder than I have allowed you to guess from my letters. There was no actual need to do away with him. Where shall I look for a defense?

At the moment the only defense I can think of is simply this—the captain knows I killed him!

Even as I write this, I hear his footsteps above me, as I heard them when I sat here composing my first letter to you. He is dressing for dinner. We are to dine together at Romano's.

And there, my lady, you have finally the answer to the mystery that has—I hope—puzzled you. I killed my friend the captain in my second letter to you, and all the odd developments that followed lived only in my imagination as I sat here beside the green-shaded lamp in my study, plotting how I should write seven letters to you that would, as the novel advertisements say, grip your attention to the very end. Oh, I am guilty—there is no denying that. And, though I do not wish to ape old Adam and imply that I was tempted by a lovely woman, a strict regard for the truth forces me to add that there is also guilt upon your head. How so? Go back to that message you inserted in the Daily Mail: "The grapefruit lady's great fondness for mystery and romance—"

You did not know it, of course; but in those words you passed me a challenge I could not resist; for making plots is the business of life—more, the breath of life—to me. I have made many; and perhaps you have followed some of them, on

Broadway. Perhaps you have seen a play of mine announced for early production in London. There was mention of it in the program at the Palace. That was the business which kept me in England. The project has been abandoned now and I am free to go back home.

Thus you see that when you granted me the privilege of those seven letters you played into my hands. So, said I, she longs for mystery and romance. Then, by the Lord Harry, she shall have them!

And it was the tramp of Captain Fraser-Freer's boots above my head that showed me the way. A fine, stalwart, cordial fellow—the captain—who has been very kind to me since I presented my letter of introduction from his cousin, Archibald Enwright. Poor Archie! A meek, correct little soul, who would be horrified beyond expression if he knew that of him I had made a spy and a frequenter of Limehouse!

The dim beginnings of the plot were in my mind when I wrote that first letter, suggesting that all was not regular in the matter of Archie's note of introduction. Before I wrote my second, I knew that nothing but the death of Fraser-Freer would do me. I recalled that Indian knife I had seen upon his desk, and from that moment he was doomed. At that time I had no idea how I should solve the mystery. But I had read and wondered at those four strange messages in the Mail, and I resolved that they must figure in the scheme of things.

The fourth letter presented difficulties until I returned from dinner that night and saw a taxi waiting before our quiet house. Hence the visit of the woman with the lilac perfume. I am afraid the Wilhelmstrasse would have little use for a lady spy who advertised herself in so foolish a manner. Time for writing the fifth letter arrived. I felt that I should now be placed under arrest. I had a faint little hope that you would be sorry about that. Oh, I'm a brute, I know!

Early in the game I had told the captain of the cruel way in which I had disposed of him. He was much amused; but he insisted, absolutely, that he must be vindicated before the close of the series, and I was with him there. He had been so bully about it all. A chance remark of his gave me my solution. He said he had it on good authority that the chief of the Czar's bureau for capturing spies in Russia was himself a spy. And so—why not a spy in Scotland Yard?

I assure you, I am most contrite as I set all this down here. You must remember that when I began my story there was no idea of war. Now all Europe is aflame; and in the face of the great conflict, the awful suffering to come, I and my little plot begin to look—well, I fancy you know just how we look.

Forgive me. I am afraid I can never find the words to tell you how important it seemed to interest you in my letters—to make you feel that I am an entertaining person worthy of your notice. That morning when you entered the Carlton breakfast room was really the biggest in my life. I felt as though you had brought with you through that doorway—But I have no right to say it. I have the right to say nothing save that now—it is all left to you. If I have offended, then I shall never hear from you again.

The captain will be here in a moment. It is near the hour set and he is never late. He is not to return to India, but expects to be drafted for the Expeditionary Force that will be sent to the Continent. I hope the German Army will be kinder to him than I was!

My name is Geoffrey West. I live at nineteen Adelphi Terrace—in rooms that look down on the most wonderful garden in London. That, at least, is real. It is very quiet there to-night, with the city and its continuous hum of war and terror seemingly a million miles away.

Shall we meet at last? The answer rests entirely with you. But, believe me, I shall be anxiously waiting to know; and if you decide to give me a chance to explain—to denounce myself to you in person—then a happy man will say good-by to this garden and these dim dusty rooms and follow you to the ends of the earth—aye, to Texas itself!

Captain Fraser-Freer is coming down the stairs. Is this good-by forever, my lady? With all my soul, I hope not.
YOUR CONTRITE STRAWBERRY MAN.

CHAPTER NINE

Words are futile things with which to attempt a description of the feelings of the girl at the Carlton as she read this, the last letter of seven written to her through the medium of her maid, Sadie Haight. Turning the pages of the dictionary casually, one might enlist a few—for example, amazement, anger, unbelief, wonder. Perhaps, to go back to the letter a, even amusement. We may leave her with the solution to the puzzle in her hand, the Saronia a little more than a day away, and a weirdly mixed company of emotions struggling in her soul.

And leaving her thus, let us go back to Adelphi Terrace and a young man exceedingly worried.

Once he knew that his letter was delivered, Mr. Geoffrey West took his place most humbly on the anxious seat. There he writhed through the long hours of Wednesday morning. Not to prolong this painful picture, let us hasten to add that at three o'clock that same afternoon came a telegram that was to end suspense. He tore it open and read:

STRAWBERRY MAN: I shall never, never forgive, you. But we are sailing tomorrow on the Saronia. Were you thinking of going home soon? MARIAN A. LARNED.

Thus it happened that, a few minutes later, to the crowd of troubled Americans in a certain steamship booking office there was added a wild-eyed young man who further upset all who saw him. To weary clerks he proclaimed in fiery tones that he must sail on the Saronia. There seemed to be no way of appeasing him. The offer of a private liner would not have interested him.

He raved and tore his hair. He ranted. All to no avail. There was, in plain American, "nothing doing!"

Damp but determined, he sought among the crowd for one who had bookings on the Saronia. He could find, at first, no one so lucky; but finally he ran across Tommy Gray. Gray, an old friend, admitted when pressed that he had a passage on that most desirable boat. But the offer of all the king's horses and all the king's gold left him unmoved. Much, he said, as he would have liked to oblige, he and his wife were determined. They would sail.

It was then that Geoffrey West made a compact with his friend. He secured from him the necessary steamer labels and it was arranged that his baggage was to go aboard the Saronia as the property of Gray.

"But," protested Gray, "even suppose you do put this through; suppose you do manage to sail without a ticket—where will you sleep? In chains somewhere below, I fancy."

"No matter!" bubbled West. "I'll sleep in the dining saloon, in a lifeboat, on the lee scuppers—whatever they are. I'll sleep in the air, without any visible support! I'll sleep anywhere—nowhere—but I'll sail! And as for irons—they don't make 'em strong enough to hold me."

At five o'clock on Thursday afternoon the Saronia slipped smoothly away from a Liverpool dock. Twenty-five hundred Americans—about twice the number the boat could comfortably carry—stood on her decks and cheered. Some of those in that crowd who had millions of money were booked for the steerage. All of them were destined to experience during that crossing hunger, annoyance, discomfort. They were to be stepped on, sat on, crowded and jostled. They suspected as much when the boat left the dock. Yet they cheered!

Gayest among them was Geoffrey West, triumphant amid the confusion. He was safely aboard; the boat was on its way! Little did it trouble him that he went as a stowaway, since he had no ticket; nothing but an overwhelming determination to be on the good ship Saronia.

That night as the Saronia stole along with all deck lights out and every porthole curtained, West saw on the dim deck the slight figure of a girl who meant much to him. She was standing staring out over the black waters; and, with wildly beating heart, he approached her, not knowing what to say, but feeling that a start must be made somehow.

"Please pardon me for addressing—" he began. "But I want to tell you—"

She turned, startled; and then smiled an odd little smile, which he could not see in the dark.

"I beg your pardon," she said. "I haven't met you, that I recall—"

"I know," he answered. "That's going to be arranged to-morrow. Mrs. Tommy Gray says you crossed with them—"

"Mere steamer acquaintances," the girl replied coldly.

"Of course! But Mrs. Gray is a darling—she'll fix that all right. I just want to say, before to-morrow comes—"

"Wouldn't it be better to wait?"

"I can't! I'm on this ship without a ticket. I've got to go down in a minute and tell the purser that. Maybe he'll throw me overboard; maybe he'll lock me up. I don't know what they do with people like me. Maybe they'll make a stoker of me. And then I shall have to stoke, with no chance of seeing you again. So that's why I want to say now—I'm sorry I have such a keen imagination. It carried me away—really it did! I didn't mean to deceive you with those letters; but, once I got started—You know, don't you, that I love you with all my heart? From the moment you came into the Carlton that morning I—"

"Really—Mr.—Mr.—"

"West—Geoffrey West. I adore you! What can I do to prove it? I'm going to prove it—before this ship docks in the North River. Perhaps I'd better talk to your father, and tell him about the Agony Column and those seven letters—"

"You'd better not! He's in a terribly bad humor. The dinner was awful, and the steward said we'd be looking back to it and calling it a banquet before the voyage ends. Then, too, poor dad says he simply can not sleep in the stateroom they've given him—"

"All the better! I'll see him at once. If he stands for me now he'll stand for me any time! And, before I go down and beard a harsh-looking purser in his den, won't you believe me when I say I'm deeply in love—"

"In love with mystery and romance! In love with your own remarkable powers of invention! Really, I can't take you seriously—"

"Before this voyage is ended you'll have to. I'll prove to you that I care. If the purser lets me go free—"

"You have much to prove," the girl smiled. "To-morrow— when Mrs. Tommy Gray introduces us—I may accept you—as a builder of plots. I happen to know you are good. But—as—It's too silly! Better go and have it out with that purser."

Reluctantly he went. In five minutes he was back. The girl was still standing by the rail.

"It's all right!" West said. "I thought I was doing something original, but there were eleven other people in the same fix. One of them is a billionaire from Wall Street. The purser collected some money from us and told us to sleep on the deck—if we could find room."

"I'm sorry," said the girl. "I rather fancied you in the role of stoker." She glanced about her at the dim deck. "Isn't this exciting? I'm sure this voyage is going to be filled with mystery and romance."

"I know it will be full of romance," West answered. "And the mystery will be—can I convince you—"

"Hush!" broke in the girl. "Here comes father! I shall be very happy to meet you—to-morrow. Poor dad! he's looking for a place to sleep."

Five days later poor dad, having slept each night on deck in his clothes while the ship plowed through a cold drizzle, and having starved in a sadly depleted dining saloon, was a sight to move the heart of a political opponent. Immediately after a dinner that had scarcely satisfied a healthy Texas appetite he lounged gloomily in the deck chair which was now his stateroom. Jauntily Geoffrey West came and sat at his side.

"Mr. Larned," he said, "I've got something for you."

And, with a kindly smile, he took from his pocket and handed over a large, warm baked potato. The Texan eagerly accepted the gift.

"Where'd you get it?" he demanded, breaking open his treasure.

"That's a secret," West answered. "But I can get as many as I want. Mr. Larned, I can say this—you will not go hungry any longer. And there's something else I ought to speak of. I am sort of aiming to marry your daughter."

Deep in his potato the Congressman spoke:

"What does she say about it?"

"Oh, she says there isn't a chance. But—"

"Then look out, my boy! She's made up her mind to have you."

"I'm glad to hear you say that. I really ought to tell you who I am. Also, I want you to know that, before your daughter and I met, I wrote her seven letters—"

"One minute," broke in the Texan. "Before you go into all that, won't you be a good fellow and tell me where you got this potato?"

West nodded.

"Sure!" he said; and, leaning over, he whispered.

For the first time in days a smile appeared on the face of the older man.

"My boy," he said, "I feel I'm going to like you. Never mind the rest. I heard all about you from your friend Gray; and as for those letters—they were the only thing that made the first part of this trip bearable. Marian gave them to me to read the night we came on board."

Suddenly from out of the clouds a long-lost moon appeared, and bathed that over-crowded ocean liner in a flood of silver. West left the old man to his potato and went to find the daughter.

She was standing in the moonlight by the rail of the forward deck, her eyes staring dreamily ahead toward the great country that had sent her forth light-heartedly for to adventure and to see. She turned as West came up.

"I have just been talking with your father," he said. "He tells me he thinks you mean to take me, after all."

She laughed. "To-morrow night," she answered, "will be our last on board. I shall give you my final decision then."

"But that is twenty-four hours away! Must I wait so long as that?"

"A little suspense won't hurt you. I can't forget those long days when I waited for your letters—"

"I know! But can't you give me—just a little hint—here—to-night?"

"I am without mercy—absolutely without mercy!"

And then, as West's fingers closed over her hand, she added softly: "Not even the suspicion of a hint, my dear—except to tell you that—my answer will be—yes."

THE END

If you've enjoyed this book, you will not want to miss these terrific titles…

ARMCHAIR SCI-FI & MYSTERY CLASSICS, $12.95 each

C-40 **MODEL FOR MURDER**
by Stephen Marlowe

C-41 **PRELUDE TO MURDER**
by Sterling Noel

C-42 **DEAD WEIGHT**
by Frank Kane

C-43 **A DAME CALLED MURDER**
by Milton Ozaki

C-44 **THE GREATEST ADVENTURE**
by John Taine

C-45 **THE EXILE OF TIME**
by Ray Cummings

C-46 **STORM OVER WARLOCK**
by Andre Norton

C-47 **MAN OF MANY MINDS**
by E. Everett Evans

C-48 **THE GODS OF MARS**
by Edgar Rice Burroughs

C-49 **BRIGANDS OF THE MOON**
by Ray Cummings

C-50 **SPACE HOUNDS OF IPC**
by E. E. "Doc" Smith

C-51 **THE LANI PEOPLE**
J. F. Bone

C-52 **THE MOON POOL**
by A. Merritt

C-53 **IN THE DAYS OF THE COMET**
by H. G. Wells

C-54 **TRIPLANETARY**
C. C. Doc Smith

If you've enjoyed this book, you will not want to miss these terrific titles…

ARMCHAIR SCI-FI & HORROR DOUBLE NOVELS, $12.95 each

If you've enjoyed this book, you will not want to miss these terrific titles…

ARMCHAIR SCI-FI & HORROR DOUBLE NOVELS, $12.95 each

D-71   **THE DEEP END** by Gregory Luce
TO WATCH BY NIGHT by Robert Moore Williams

D-72   **SWORDSMAN OF LOST TERRA** by Poul Anderson
PLANET OF GHOSTS by David V. Reed

D-73   **MOON OF BATTLE** by J. J. Allerton
THE MUTANT WEAPON by Murray Leinster

D-74   **OLD SPACEMEN NEVER DIE!** John Jakes
RETURN TO EARTH by Bryan Berry

D-75   **THE THING FROM UNDERNEATH** by Milton Lesser
OPERATION INTERSTELLAR by George O. Smith

D-76   **THE BURNING WORLD** by Algis Budrys
FOREVER IS TOO LONG by Chester S. Geier

D-77   **THE COSMIC JUNKMAN** by Rog Phillips
THE ULTIMATE WEAPON by John W. Campbell

D-78   **THE TIES OF EARTH** by James H. Schmitz
CUE FOR QUIET by Thomas L. Sherred

D-79   **SECRET OF THE MARTIANS** by Paul W. Fairman
THE VARIABLE MAN by Philip K. Dick

D-80   **THE GREEN GIRL** by Jack Williamson
THE ROBOT PERIL by Don Wilcox

ARMCHAIR SCIENCE FICTION CLASSICS, $12.95 each

C-25   **THE STAR KINGS**
by Edmond Hamilton

C-26   **NOT IN SOLITUDE**
by Kenneth Gantz

C-32   **PROMETHEUS II**
by S. J. Byrne

ARMCHAIR SCI-FI & HORROR GEMS SERIES, $12.95 each

G-7   **SCIENCE FICTION GEMS, Vol. Seven**
Jack Sharkey and others

G-8   **HORROR GEMS, Vol. Eight**
Seabury Quinn and others

Made in the USA
Middletown, DE
13 June 2020